Middle-Aged Man in a Trashcan

by

William Brian Johnson

Cover Art by *Teddi Black*

The Wild Rose Press, Inc.
PO Box 708
Adams Basin, NY 14410-0708
Visit us at www.thewildrosepress.com

Publishing History
First Edition, 2025
Trade Paperback ISBN 978-1-5092-6150-5
Digital ISBN 978-1-5092-6151-2

Published in the United States of America

Dedication

For Connor, Justin, and Alex – These are our many worlds.

Chapter 1

There are rules for a new world. Peek out of the trash can and watch for anything odd. People that walk with a limp and look dead, dragons, lizardfolk that hide in the shadows. Or in the most dangerous worlds, the little girl with the bottomless black eyes that won't stop staring at you when all life around her is gone.

This world smells like burning metal and feels a little warm to the touch. That's a bad sign. The first peek shows an orange sky like we're in the middle of a forest fire. The second peek shows a typical empty alley with a ton of full trash receptacles. Another bad sign was no one had picked up trash in a while. No dragons or lizard people, check. Hot air blew in like a windy summer day, odd because it's early spring. The hot wind doesn't help with the sour tang and sickly-sweet smell of trash.

People scream in the distance. That's a no-go.

"Nobuyuki, be careful. It's on fire." A white flash of supernatural fur flew up my back and out. They disappear over the high-rise building within seconds.

Nobuyuki is my companion on this journey. They get all the pronouns depending on mood and form, and knows what to do in new worlds because we have a system worked out. One that we don't always remember or follow.

Nobuyuki is a beautiful, white three-tailed fox. Fox as in the animal, three-tailed as in something from folklore. A talking multi-dimensional fox, and only a fox part-time. When I get lazy and shorten their name to Yuki, the Japanese word for snow, they get mad. But we're all a little mad down here. We float on a multidimensional current into lands of the unknown.

There's too much smoke, that's a no-go. I shut the lid and I wait in the confines of my sixth-dimensional space. My weird interdimensional pocket where eternity projects like a map of the universe staked on top of an infinite number of clear maps that rotate in and out of sight. Of which, I have no control where it goes.

In the void, I must be careful while waiting on Nobuyuki. If I stare at a point too long, my interdimensional space moves and I lose Nobuyuki. I close my eyes and my mind and wait for the thump. There are gaps in my memory. Sometimes I remember the last couple months, sometimes I can't remember the day before. Nobuyuki calls it brain trauma and my memories will come back in time.

Thump. Nobuyuki slips in and we go over our checklist in the dark.

"Are people on the street?" I ask.

"Yes, but not many. Something terrible is happening." Their tinny voice sounds like someone pushed the treble up on the stereo.

"Military?"

"No, but police cars with lights flashing. No military," Nobuyuki answers.

"Screaming?"

There is a sigh in the multiverse dark. "No one is screaming at the moment, but everyone's tense." Someone screams off in the distance.

"Authoritarian statues or flags?"

"Joe." The voice is suddenly older. Nobuyuki takes the old man form. They tire of the constant questions and it's the only voice I listen to. "No strange statues that seem too big or flags. No lizard people, dragons, or floating ancients."

"Good, I don't want to repeat any of that." I take a deep breath. "We failed some checks. What's with the orange sky?"

"Wildfires to the east of the city. They look bad. Are you ready, Joe?"

"Is it dangerous?" I ask. We've been in the void for too long, the last worlds were trash and we didn't stay. We've traveled a long way and this is a rest stop, but it's a rest stop with no lights and a large windowless van idling nearby. The wanderlust has set in and we need to stretch our legs, as long as death isn't immediate. There is silence in the void and the old man knows I hate it. "Fine. Check the alley."

Nobuyuki passes me and out the top.

"There is no one looking," Nobuyuki says.

Air always smells different. The atmosphere tingles and crawls up my skin. It's like walking into someone's home for the first time, no one else understands the scent or the feel, but the newcomer. Nobuyuki calls it "dimensional shift" and you just need to let the dimension settle in around you and take you in. The old man hasn't mentioned dimensional rejection…yet.

Burning metal is a smell you don't forget and smoke seems everywhere. I take another deep breath of new dimension air and do my best to gracefully step out of the trash receptacle. Sometimes it's easy. Sometimes I knock over the entire thing.

"Joe?" I turn to see a bald Japanese man in his

seventies standing in traditional Japanese robes. I misstep and fall. It elicits a laugh as I pick myself off the warm pavement.

"That's odd, pavement's hot like it's summer." I look up at the building next to us.

Memories come in bursts then fall apart like trying to grab smoke.

"Where are we?"

"Fort Wayne, Indiana, you idiot. Apparently not a good version of it," the old man replies. "But I'm cooped up and want to explore."

"No immediate danger?"

He walks down the alley with the grace of a trained Aikido master. I look homeless. When Nobuyuki transforms every hair is in place and the illusion is flawless. I looked stained. I haven't showered in a long time, my beard is long, and I don't own a comb. Sometimes it's handy because Nobuyuki gets all the attention either like this or in a young girl's form. I'm invisible and okay with that. At least this time, I'm not covered in blood.

The old man pauses. "Let's see what's going on before we rush to the next place."

People are out and panicked. You see someone staring down death a few times and it's easy to figure out.

"This is a bad place, Nobuyuki."

The old man stops before me and nods to the east. "Look."

Through the wildfire's smoke, mountains of loose rock rise above the horizon. Something in my head stammers it's the moon. It scrapes the atmosphere trailing burning moondust. I'm in the middle of a boiling tea kettle with a 747 flying mere feet overhead. That elevator big drop feeling hits my stomach, not down but sideways in a fierce tidal pull.

It roars across the sky as the storm sirens blare. People scream too and it all blends together in an overwhelming squelch. The panic-stricken bolt through the street and all head to a similar place. I grab Nobuyuki in the chaos and drag him with the flood of humanity. Booms constantly thunder throughout the atmosphere as moondust and rocks enter the atmosphere.

"We should head back," Nobuyuki says.

I'm a panicked lemming in the surge. Nobuyuki separates from me. The shattered moon's orbit takes up the sky and eclipses daylight. The large rocks closest to Earth melt as it scrapes the upper atmosphere. There's the sound and heat of sizzling fajitas along with the smell that it cooked too long. It burns my throat. I stop and stare as people surge around me. Moon bits, satellites, and space stations decelerate and explode like meteorites. The moon's a gigantic plow taking everything out in its path.

The stream of humanity crushes and forces me forward. Fireballs rocket overhead, emitting thundering sonic booms that punch the guts and shake the ground. Glass is raining down all around us from the tall buildings. A smoking chunk of metal lands not far from me. A Soviet-era flag stares out from the atmospheric soot. I stop and gawk, but can't stop with the sea of humanity behind me.

The masses rush into a squat parking structure as something explodes nearby. People are talking about the news. Tsunamis which swamped out the Eastern Seaboard months ago are moving farther inland.

Something called the Roche Limit is tossed around like its meaning should be known.

People talk about running and the discussion shuts down when they talk about where. This is the End of Days. Or from the moon's last pass, the End of Day.

There are familiar faces in the shelter. Familiar like you waved at someone, then when you get close, you realize it's not them. Subtle changes, the guard's name and nationality are different. Maybe he changed to blond and added or subtracted fifty pounds. One in the crowd always draws my attention. I always find Rebecca. She's a familiar: a person in the multiverses that appears roughly the same. She's been a waitress, a police officer, lizard cult leader, military captain, and lover. Nobuyuki says it happens from time to time in a nexus. The multiverse plains are close enough together that some people just don't change much.

"Are you open for business today, Tom?" someone shouts.

There is a pause and a laugh. "We're always open for business," someone answers back. "Even today."

Nobuyuki looks annoyed.

It's a calm voice in this maelstrom of emotions as another piece of debris crashes nearby. Several soul-shaking booms outside, then a steady whistle getting louder, incoming. People are pushing to get in when it happens. It hits, we're covered in choking dust, rumbles, and the sky falls. The structure cracks and groans. The dust cakes my eyes as someone grabs me. We move fast.

"We need to go. This is a bad place." I'm picked up by the old man. "Stop rubbing your eyes or you will injure yourself."

He runs with me like an old martial arts master.

Jumping up debris, fires, and incoming objects with a flip and a kick. People watch us not knowing what to think. Sadly, it won't matter.

Nobuyuki pauses for a moment, then moves impossibly fast. We're surrounded by fire. We move through it and away.

There's mist in the air. Nobuyuki stops and sets me down. He takes my hand and puts it into cold water. I cup it and wash out my eyes. It hurts. I force my eyes open to see. I'm near a broken fire hydrant and water is everywhere. Nobuyuki rushes down the street. I blink a few times to clear the dust.

Overhead, a fireball flairs to life and falls toward the Indiana Michigan Power Center where my cart is. Nobuyuki folds like a piece of origami and disappears with a pop. It's a small local dimensional jump. He does that, I can't.

The fireball hits the building near where we left the trash cart causing the upper level to fall on itself. The building falls into the alley. This is it.

Dust and smoke fill the street and softly envelops everything. I huddle, not being able to see in front of me, and pull my T-shirt over my face. It doesn't work and I'm choking on dust. Papers are floating down in the debris. A few of us stand around and watch. There's a prairie dog mentality to observe the end. There's nowhere to run and no sense of search and rescue on a doomed ship.

The orange glow of fire brightens the eastern sky, highlighting a cityscape that's missing teeth. Several of the buildings that make the skyline are gone or busted. The Indiana Michigan Power Center, the highest point in the city, is missing its top layers. The cart is in the alley, crushed by the upper levels.

"Nobuyuki," I whisper.

We're living the summer blockbuster disaster movie. I'm far from the square-jawed actor ready to save the world. I'm more of the fluffy middle-aged guy who buys it horribly in the first act.

There are gaps in the Indiana Michigan Power Center. Out of the skyscraper, glass, steel, and concrete fall. My eyes and chest burn, but I have to find Nobuyuki. Our group of prairie dogs move like a herd. The heat is palatable from this place. Dust moves toward the wildfire's glow like a big vacuum. The dust moves slow, maybe the fire isn't as close as it feels.

The alleyway we came out of now is a hill of debris. Someone in the crowd mentions ninety minutes. I look up and see the moon is already setting.

"Ninety minutes before this again?" I ask.

People look at me like I'm out of my mind.

"It gets closer, but ninety minutes, yeah. You're not from around here, are you, traveler?" The young Mexican guy from the parking garage is studying me. He recognizes something's off. He's wearing a "Sancho Tom, Tacos, Love, and Happiness" shirt. It's a young Mexican guy I've seen around. He must be another familiar. "Nothing else is falling and we have ninety minutes before it starts again. You know, because of the moon's orbit."

He drones like I'm back in elementary school and not getting the lesson. I've got ninety minutes to find Nobuyuki and get out of here. Orange sky and fire everywhere are on the list of "no-goes" if we survive. Our group of prairie dogs fan out, downgrading our chance of survival. Sancho Tom seems like he's waiting

8

for me to do something. I walk to the alleyway. He follows.

"You're not making it in that way," he says.

I turn and look at him. "A friend of mine ran into the alley."

"The old man?" he replies, shaking his head.

"I got to get him out. There's something we need in there," I shouldn't be talking but the shock of it all has turned off my filter.

He talks and I look at the alleyway. There is a small trucking entrance on the east side. This side was a no-go.

I walk around the ruins of the building.

"Hey, my name's Tom." He puts out his hand.

It took me out of my plan.

"Do I know you?" I don't put my hand out and run around the building, leaving him behind.

"No, but you do and you will," he calls behind me.

I'm winded. There's too much junk in the air. Large slabs of concrete fall from the building as I make it to the front park. I trot around the rest of the building between deep breaths and coughing fits. Someone is there.

"Tom?"

"Hey."

Tom's standing in front of tons of crumbled concrete in the alleyway, looking at it like a fresh cut yard. *How did he get here so fast?*

"There are shortcuts everywhere, man."

Tom's following me and I don't have time for this.

"Listen. I know you're worried about your friend and whatever you need to do here is impossible. Let me help you," Tom says, turns to me, and arches an eyebrow. "So you can go home."

I stare at him and shrug. "What can you do?"

9

"Help you not make stupid decisions and get out of here." He sticks his hand out again for me to take.

"My life is the sum of stupid decisions." Tom wants something, but I take his hand. As our hands connect, weird energy shoots up my arm like I struck a nerve.

"That's what I thought, traveler. In another time and place, we need to have a long talk."

The electricity. Tom might be a traveler too. "This is what we're going to do. You're going to walk next to me, my hand's going to be on your shoulder, and we can't break contact. You got that? We cannot break contact."

"Um, sure?" I shrug.

He stares into my eyes. "If you break contact you die. Say it again."

"Don't break contact," I repeat. He scares me a little with the intensity. Tom takes a deep breath, moves next to me, and touches my shoulder. The world changes. The sun is out. It is a gorgeous day. There is no debris. I shrug off his touch and return to the hellish landscape.

"Hey. What did I say?"

Back in school again. "Sorry, don't break contact or I die. I wasn't ready for that."

We moved in the brief contact. We're in between debris piles. Large slabs of concrete create an odd shelter against the perimeter wall.

"What are you?"

"I'm help, Joe."

"I didn't tell you who I was."

"I know. This isn't the spacetime to have this conversation. You need help. Let me help you. You can help me at a later time."

I bet the Devil says the same thing before. He

touches me and we shift closer. I don't like his calmness and the odd air that he's not in mortal danger. Reality is changing with heartbeats. We're inside the building somewhere else. Now it's raining outside. It shifts and we're by the door that leads to the alleyway and it looks like a hurricane outside. Then he lets go. We're back. There's a gap in the ruined wall and a small patch of dirty white robe in the rubble.

"Nobuyuki!" I shout.

"He's under all that. Let me help you."

We shift and there's a shadow on the ground where Nobuyuki is. We back into the gap and he lets go.

He's looking at Nobuyuki's male form but somehow knows and hesitates. Dust is in the air and subtle groans announce through the structure. I try to climb through the broken window.

"Don't let your emotions get in the way, or you're going to get stuck too." He rushes forward and grabs me in a half-shoulder hug. We're back in the light and clean building. A short, professionally dressed brunette screams and runs back into a wall, dropping the papers she had in her hand.

"Sorry, Sarah. Didn't mean to spook you." Tom forces me forward. I'm a dusty homeless guy in an odd hug with a clean-cut kid forcibly led down the hall. She scatters like a scared lizard. "We gotta move before security comes down on us."

We half run down the hall to the door in a weird four-legged race. Out in the alley, there is a line of trash carts. Tom half drags me to them, slapping the tops of them as we move.

"Duck, duck…goose. This is it." It's the one. Spacetime hums around me.

"Nobuyuki?"

"You won't like this. Don't move."

Tom makes a step sideways, an odd rotation where the world seems to freeze, go out of frame, and the hellish skyscape returns over the clean office building. We're on an interdimensional rollercoaster with all the loops and spins. I want to vomit but don't know what will happen if I do. We're standing in the ghost of debris. I'm holding tight to Tom but a steel beam rests through my head.

"Don't let go and move with me," Tom says, his voice watery.

We shift forward and the world lags behind us. I can't process it and do my best not to pass out as the world spins.

"Here." Tom drags me forward. Ghosts are watching us. I want to ask questions but everything is so discombobulated. We pass through debris. An odd shape walks toward us as others run away. There's a void in the ground. As we pass the darkened bubble, Nobuyuki is on the ground. Tom touches Nobuyuki as they transform into their three-tailed fox form. "Ewww. I thought so," Tom says as he picks them up then tightens the grip on me. "We need to move, buddy."

The horizon isn't lining up, I have a grip on the trash cart, it feels squishy. Reality is squishy. I'm falling through reality.

"I got you," Tom says. I look at him and see another Tom standing calmly pointing in another direction.

For a moment, I witness every reality at once. Tom is there, everywhere. My mind can't take it and everything goes black.

****

I come to. We're in the park section in front of the building. Nobuyuki's passed out in my lap. The trash cart's crushed, but part of it is supporting us. The orange sky has returned. Tom sits on one of the concrete tree planters, tapping me with his foot.

"I'd let you sleep, but the end is nigh," Tom says flatly.

The atmosphere roars like a jet on low approach, my stomach feels yanked to the left, and the moon emerges as hot wind spreads embers into the city.

"This is it, bud. This is the end of this world." He takes my hand and taps the side of the trash cart with it. I'm still in a stupor as the cart pops itself back into a normal shape. Tom opens the lid. Purple light escapes from inside. Tom looks in and smiles. "Cool," I think he says.

The streets are empty and the buildings are on fire.

"Our little trip took longer than I expected. This is the last orbit."

Tom stands. I close the trash cart lid and lay Nobuyuki on it. They're breathing in deep slow breaths. Nobuyuki's normal white is gone, dirtied by the soot and ash. She's a dark splotch moving into darkness.

"It'll be okay, but buddy, we need to have a serious chat about your choice of companions." Tom stares at Nobuyuki. "You will find me again."

"Who are you?"

His eyebrows knit together while he stares at Nobuyuki. It passes as he looks back at me. He smiles probably one of the only smiles at the End of Days. "I'm Sancho Tom, a friend you're going to see from time to time. Now watch." His hand goes out like a ringmaster diverting attention from the dancing elephants to the clowns.

A man crosses the park toward us, away from the rubble's protection. He's bloody, his suit is ripped and on fire. I lose focus on the trash can and the light dies out.

"Should we help him?"

"From the Apocalypse? Nah." Tom shakes his head as embers rain down hard around us. There is a low rumble to the east of us. The wind is getting stronger. The suited man is having more difficulty. His shuffling walk has turned into a drunken stumble.

"He's dying, but soon enough, everyone will," Tom says.

The man shuffles his feet and falls to his knees. The wind overpowers what he pleads. His face warps like it's made of wax and melts. His arm reaches out and sheds its skin. Underneath a fog-like substance creates his form with lightning running back and forth. He crawls on the ground and the odd skin glows and fades. A hard wind knocks him over. Followed by darkness as the moon snuffs out the sun. Lightning outlines a nervous system. His face falls off, hits the ground, and shatters. The gray mist-like form relaxes and all light fades from it. The rest of "him" disintegrates the fog-like form and blows with the embers down the street. His now empty clothes ball up and threaten to tumbleweed away.

"What the hell?" I yell.

The winds increase. Embers whip and fly like stars passing at warp speed. The building protecting us fails. "Time to go, Joe. I'll see you on the other side." Tom picks up Nobuyuki and opens the trash cart. The heat becomes unbearable as debris falls nearby.

The heat is stopping me from making the portal. He

takes a long look at Nobuyuki. He taps the trash cart a couple of times until my familiar glow comes out and drops them in. How in the hell did he do that? Our skin scorches.

"There is a wall of fire and force entering Fort Wayne, Indiana, that nothing will survive. You better go," he says.

Buildings are flying apart in the distance like in the warm embrace from a nuclear blast.

"What about you? Are you coming?" I'm practically yelling this above the noise.

"Nah, I can't. If I enter the void, that would be bad. Like taking this and spreading it everywhere. I'll be fine. Look for my taco truck in the next world. I'm sure business will be better and I'll have regular hours."

He speaks at a normal level above the world's cries, but I easily hear them. Tom removes his T-shirt and throws it at me as I move into the cart. He's got a taco tattooed on his chest over a Mayan calendar. His skin blisters and burns like it's under a broiler.

I grab the T-shirt and climb in stealing a look at the body on the ground. The clothes blew away and there is only emptiness. Tom walks out to the street and spreads his arms in a T-pose like he's sunbathing. I'm watching him die.

I look to the east. It's all fire. "It's beautiful."

"It always is, Joe. See you in the next life." I shut the lid and fall into the portal, moving in the larger dimensional shift.

I'm smoldering, blistered, and singed. The wind above the lid roars like a jet threatening to rip the cover off, then we move, and it falls silent. I stayed too long, but as I settle in, my skin soothes. The void recharges and heals us. It doesn't remove the burning hair smell. I'm sleepy and settle in for a long nap. Time doesn't matter so I always get to sleep in. I rub my hair and feel its charred ends falling off, relaxing and regrowing. "Too close," I murmur as I grab Nobuyuki and cuddle up watching the universe outside. They're breathing and will be fine. I watched the end and survived while meeting a new friend who died but told me he'd see me again. Eternity's darkness swallows me and I sleep.

Chapter 2

"There are rules to a new world."

The voice woke me from my fog. I glance out into darkness. I'm floating, like swimming in a pool, but I'm floating among stars, galaxies, universes. A young girl holds my head in the darkness. I stare at the shadow but see delicate features.

She smiles at me. "Hi, Joe."

I panic. I move quickly but I don't know how to. It's all reflex. I thrash in space. My body felt good but something in my mind wails that I should be in pain.

"You make up new lies to believe. Sometimes, like in your case, the mind resets and you forget everything. I'm a friend, Joe." Her small hand brushes my face. Then she glows red. I can't think. She's glowing, normal people don't glow. She's Japanese. Am I?

I back off and my hand flails out. I hit something above. Sunlight shows through the crack.

"Joe! We're not ready! Stop!" she shouts. She's now glowing yellow and it's freaking me out.

I explode out of a trash cart in an alleyway between a large L-shaped building and a brick wall and fall on my butt. I lay there for a moment trying to get my breath back. I look normal, dirty. Are my clothes burnt? They smell burnt. What happened? Where am I? I stand up and walk over to a glass door. I see myself in the reflection. Dark long hair in a cap, old green canvas military jacket, a long beard. I stare at the reflection until a young office girl walks by. She looks at me and screams. Not a good sign. I run. Something slips out of the trash cart behind me. A tiny white fox with three tails runs up the side of the L-shaped building. I'm staring stupidly as a security guard walks up.

"You're not allowed to be back here." The large security guard stares me down. I look at him and look up to the building. The fox is gone. I mumble something and point. He digs in his pocket and pulls out a strange card. It looks like shiny aluminum.

"Here, buddy. They'll take care of all your needs. Go see them now."

I take the card and grunt. There is an address here. As I touch the card, a small map appears and hovers in space above it, telling me where to go. I'm spinning around and the card is orienting. This is cool.

"Oh, boy." The guard says. He touches my shoulder and radios someone. "Come on, buddy."

He's leading me somewhere with a gentle push. "This way, I'll take you."

I clear my throat. "My name is Joe." It comes out hoarse.

"Hey, Joe. My name is Mike, and we're going to be okay."

We walk around the wall and onto the street. The state capital looks familiar, except the flag flying above it is wrong. I remember an old flag but this one is red, white, and black. White background, black cross, and a large red star in the center.

"I've been here, but that's not right."

"You must not be from around here." Mike pushes me along. The library sits past the state capitol. It seems smaller than in the past. It should be white stone, but it's polished black, almost artistic.

"I need to do research." Thoughts and panic weigh down my guts. I did this all wrong. "I'm in danger." I look at Mike. He shrugs.

"You'll be fine in here. They will help you." He pushes me up the stone steps of the library. There are guards out front. Police officers? I can't tell but they are all in black and look like military. The black helmets they wear have mirrored face shields. One approaches.

"Problem?" he says. His voice comes out of a radio.

"This guy was playing in the trash over in the Power Complex."

"State ID?"

"I didn't ask." Mike hands me over and doesn't say bye before leaving. Rude.

"We'll take care of him."

The officer grabs my arm and walks me into the building. The other guard lets him in. We're in a glass-lined entryway between the doors. The guard waves and opens the door. There are people at desks and cubicles working. No one looks up.

We enter a dark room, approach a very fine large wooden court bench. It smells like a forest and a hospital in here. The lights come on momentarily blinding me. Someone in robes and a hood is seated staring at me and the officer. I look down. We're in a silver circle inlaid into the marble floor.

"Cause?" the robed figure states.

"10-66 possible 10-59 from the Power Center." The officer rattles the numbers off while holding firmly to me."

"Plead?" The robed figure's voice dips and echoes.

It's dead silence in here. The officer knocks into my shoulder.

"Oh." I hold up the card that Mike gave me and smile.

The robed figure hits a gavel and it echoes through the room like summer thunder.

"Chamber."

A door opens to the side of the room. The lights come on and showcases a reclining black cylinder. It opens and reveals a bed and pillow that stands up and rotates towards us. A strange white jacket opens on the bed like a clamshell showing off a pearl. The officer is moving me to the machine.

"Can I leave?" I ask.

"Soon enough." The officer leads me to the chamber and puts a small device on my finger, the machine registers quick beeps. He rotates me and leans me face-first into the cylinder. The strange jacket hugs me and lowers me gently to the bed. His heavy hand holds me down until I'm completely horizontal. The cylinder takes me off my feet as it rotates. I sink onto the foam bed and can't move. There's a cut-out that my face fits through and a shiny bucket below me. He shuts the cylinder and I'm in complete darkness. The clamshell squeezes down on me almost forcing my breath out. The beeping speeds up as I strain against the jacket but it is no use. There is a loud hiss and my ears pop. I try to yell and find my voice is weak against the hiss. Something pokes my arm. My chest feels like it's on fire as something knocks outside. I'm very sleepy and it's hard to think. The beeping is slowing down.

The hissing stops. I can't breathe and it feels like something huge is crushing me. The cylinder cracks, light and air rush in. I breathe but my eyes hurt and I'm too heavy to move.

The door to the cylinder rips open and an old Japanese man is there with a sword.

"Samurai," I say as the world fades to black. Blood outlines the guard on the floor.

****

I wake up floating and in the dark. I panic for a moment but someone gently holds my head and murmurs prayers over me. There's a soft yellow light coming from the old man. We're in this same dark space again. My eyes adjust to the universes, galaxies, then stars. The old man stops.

"Nobuyuki?"

"I thought we lost you. It's good this place heals. You had a lethal injection, I barely got you back in time." Nobuyuki's glow dims among the universes as shadows crawl across their darkened features.

When he releases my head, it squeals with a headache. The old man sees my pain and takes my head in his hands. Nobuyuki's pressure makes my headache fall back into some forgotten hellish abyss. The glow returns. "This is going to take a while, friend. Sleep."

I don't have time to argue as the universe wraps around me.

Chapter 3

I open my eyes in time-space. Time never flows right in the space between. We see solar systems battle, galaxies collide, gigantic stars go nova and obliterate the near space.

"If Carl Sagan could see this," I say sleepily.

"Your Sagan can see this. He is one with the multiverse," the old man mutters as fingers press against my head. The pressure should hurt, but it clears my head. Nobuyuki's surrounded by a throbbing red glow. I realize it's in tune with my heartbeat. Nobuyuki's form darkens like they're covered in a lunar eclipse shadow.

"What happened? How do I remember Carl Sagan and not know anything from the last week?"

"Mental trauma, brain trauma, you've been at this for a while. You reset after something upsetting. We had back-to-back bad worlds where you sustained major injuries. The last world almost got you."

"I almost died?"

The old man sighs. "Yes, but up to the end, they treated you humanely." The old man lights up like a miniature star. The blast of light hurts my eyes. When I look again, the shadows have burned out of his form.

"There have been worse incidents."

He cocks an eyebrow and knows my next question.

"What—"

"Not now, Joe. We've seen some horrible things.

That's why you reset. Humans have limits."

I push the tension from my shoulders and let my head flop. This is Nobuyuki, but I know a girl by the same name.

"Where is the girl? Is she family?"

"When you are ready, friend. I'll tell you. She's fine. Don't worry."

"Sorry, I ran yesterday. I woke up and had no memory."

"Yes, the previous encounter…we barely made it out of there." He sighs. "When you recover, we must discuss the rules. Sometimes, the worlds are too familiar and invite us into disaster."

"Where—"

"It's like a list with you: What are you? Where are we? Who am I? Right?"

I float in the darkness, wondering if the old man reads minds. He smiles. He can read my mind.

"How long have I been out?" I interject so he's wrong.

"Time is irrelevant in the void. Long enough. I think you've finally flushed out the toxin." The old man removes his hands again, he maintains the glow, but there are dimmer areas on his body, almost like sunspots. The light hurts my eyes. I squint and watch him pull into a meditative position.

"Close your eyes, Joe. Look away."

I do. The light increases again. I almost yell. There is no heat, but it feels like we're swimming in starlight. My arms block my face, but it doesn't protect me. The light decreases.

"Ease up, buddy." The voice sounds different, smaller, and tinlike. "I'm clear."

For a moment, I'm blinded. Then little points of light return. I stretch out and watch the universe. It's dark in here and I can't see the old man in starlight.

"Where are you?"

"I'm here." Something settles in the darkness. He wasn't there a moment ago.

I look at a nearby solar system. When you see the cosmos, movement seems slow. Now it doesn't feel like we're moving at all.

"We've arrived."

"Who are you?"

The old man laughs in the darkness and it sounds like little chimes. He's smiling in the darkness. "I need to make a movie. This is the seventh time I've reintroduced myself."

"Seven?"

"Yeah. We've been hanging out for a while. Do you remember anything about dragons?"

"Freaking dragons?"

"Okay, you don't remember. I should have expected that. Sometimes you remember, most of the time you don't. My name is Nobuyuki."

"I remember that. Yuki?" Something smacks me and it hurts. "Ow."

"Refer to me by my full name. The shortened name is offensive."

"Okay, sorry." I hold my hands up to block another Nobuyuki punch. "You can call me Joe if that makes you feel better."

He growls in the darkness.

Nobuyuki reaches up and light cracks into our darkness.

"What are you?"

There is a groan. Something moves above me, the light shines down again and the old man looks at me. "See, nothing new." He glances out, then shuts the lid and drops back down. "We are here. I want you to look and tell me what you see. There is no hurry, as long as the lid's closed, and you won't drift us elsewhere."

"You talked about rules?"

"We've ignored them recently. It's easy. Look out and if it feels bad, we stay in here and move. We failed the time before last and went into a dangerous world. We did too many quick jumps and needed to stretch. I'm smarter now."

"So, it was your fault?" I ask. "Can we control where we go?"

"No. If we could, we would be home. At least what we could call home." His response is quick and angry. "We're so far out from where we started, I don't know where we are."

"We didn't start at the same place, did we?"

"No, we didn't. I don't think I've ever been to your world."

"Oh, you're from a world of dragons."

There is a stretch of silence in the darkness of space and it's uncomfortable. Nobuyuki sighs. "No. Back to the rules. When you first look out, look around. We should be in an alley. If not, see if we're in danger, go. If we're not in danger, shut the lid and wait. Look, listen, smell, and use your senses. If it's weird, don't touch or taste."

"Sounds good."

"I stopped paying attention to your verbal checklist a while back or I'd memorize it word for word."

"I'm ready."

"Then look." I hear it in the darkness and it's covered in sarcasm. "If you are in here alone, you can't move or I'm lost forever."

"Okay."

The old man laughs while I struggle to make it to the top. Then I bump into something. There is a crack of light. I see a normal alley as I look out. Cars pass in the distance. I watch the skyline for a moment, at least what I can see. No dragons wheeling in the sky.

I repeat my observations.

"Give it a moment." The old man sounds tinlike and small again.

I look down. He's far back in the darkness. I can't see him, but red eyes reflect up at me. I yelp and he laughs.

"Look back outside. Remember, I'm not from your world. There are differences and I'm not a 'vampire'."

That's what a vampire would say.

"Are we clear?" he asks again and I look out.

"I think." I lean forward as something rushes by. Fur brushes against me for a fleeting second. "What the Hell?" I ask in the sudden flash of light as the lid pops open, but he's gone. I don't trust opening the lid further to see where he went but leave it cracked. A few moments pass then there is a sharp knock in space. I open the lid and Nobuyuki is standing there. The old man adjusts his robes.

"Come."

I climb out noting the lack of grace, somehow the cart stays upright. We're in a clean alleyway, foot traffic echoes nearby, people walk, talk, and laugh.

"Laughter is always a good sign," Nobuyuki says.

The air feels good. It's not cold, but I cinch up my

jacket and pull down my baseball cap.

I have the feeling that no one will know me here and I'm fine with that.

"Let's go for a walk," Nobuyuki says.

We're in the shadow of the big L-shaped building and walk down the alleyway. There is a large glass door that we pass. In the building, a female office worker walks by. Glasses, hair up in a brown bun, arms full of folders. She walks by without noticing me.

"She's in a lot of our worlds. You called her a groundhog. I'm not sure why."

As we walk, I think about it. There are a couple of things it could be. My present memory of the last few years is non-existent. There are other things I remember, places, movies, books, and education. I should be a drooling baby. This big building is in my memory, the library nearby, but this is a new world. I don't remember beyond our last world. There are a couple of things that come to mind on the groundhog.

The movie Groundhog's Day, an older movie where the day repeats itself over and over. Bill Murray makes the perfect day and gets out. Problem is, I don't remember yesterday. How can I make my perfect day?

A security guard watches us walk by.

"Mike?" I whisper. He's dressed appropriately but looks completely different. I don't stop to check a name badge. He's got a wary eye on us but stands by the door, watching us walk away. Memories slip in. I didn't get grabbed. I didn't get euthanized. The gavel drops in my head and cold chills race up my spine. My heart's beating a little too fast and I need to breathe. I need to run.

"Are you okay?" Nobuyuki asks and puts a hand on my shoulder.

27

"Yeah. You said they tried to euthanize me in the last place?"

"Depends on your meaning of euthanize. It was effective and would have worked if I had gotten there any later. Your pain would have been minimal."

I try to think of anything else but that gavel drops again. Bang.

"Groundhog. It's old folklore about forcing a critter out of its hole. If it sees its shadow, it gets scared and runs away."

"Does it predict wars?"

"Weather, if I remember right. For the world."

Nobuyuki stops. I look back. He's trying to process it and it's not making sense.

"It's a tradition."

"Oh," he passes it off and walks with me.

"Maybe she's my groundhog. If she's startled, bad things are afoot."

"Does she look different?"

"She looked familiar."

"You called them familiars before," Nobuyuki says.

"Familiar?"

"Something that appears nearly the same no matter where we end up. You always recognize a few."

The alley opens into the street. It looks different here. My memory, or lack thereof, says things are in the wrong place. The skyline looks different but still functions the same. The L-shaped building is taller.

"Michigan Power Building," I read aloud. "Are we in Michigan?"

Nobuyuki sighs.

"We're not in Michigan, are we?"

"This is Fort Wayne, Indiana. Sometimes the name

changes, but we are always in the same place. Even the river's name and shape change. Which was odd, before I met you, rivers always had the same name. I used to believe that was their spirit talking." Nobuyuki stares at the ground going through memories I wish I had. "At least that's what we were taught." Nobuyuki trails off and looks to the horizon.

"You mentioned we met through a dragon?"

The old man's mouth turns up a little. "Not through a dragon. That would have been if he ate us with a most unfortunate digestive outcome." Nobuyuki laughs. "The dragon had me and was ready to eat. Then you come walking by. You're in a state. The entire city is in ruins and here you are walking around like a tourist pulling your trash cart. The hum of the wheels takes the dragon's attention off me and puts it on you. You were the better meal. It gives me time to use the sword and dispatch the dragon."

"Nobuyuki. Noble dragon slayer."

"Hmmm, noble." Nobuyuki shields a laugh. "It was a young dragon, but already working up to be a tyrant. Dragons feel if one of their own is in danger and I killed this one quickly. We heard its mother's cries clear across the city. We knew we were in danger. You grabbed me, threw me in the trash cart, and here we are."

"How long ago was that?"

"Time is the grand illusion. We appear here on the same day and time."

We find the river and a small park nearby. I find a bench and sit.

Nobuyuki sits on the ground. "Time passes. We always arrive on the same day, but luckily time passes normally when we are in a new place."

"How long have we stayed in places?"

"Moments for some. Lifetimes in others." His voice cracks. He's watching the river, thinking. Then answers my question before I ask it.

"Five years is an estimate. You mark holidays and that's my gauge. I don't know if time moves in the space but when we arrive mid-Spring, every place we end up on March 14th. Might be a fierce winter or boiling summer when we go in, then when we pop out, there are flowering buds on trees, and the local kami can't make up their mind. It's spring eternal." He places his palms flat on the grass. "The kami are happy today. This is a good place."

"Kami?"

"Local nature spirits."

"Have we stayed long anywhere?" I ask again.

"Yes." Nobuyuki flinches and stares at the river in deep thought.

"I have a feeling that's a question I shouldn't ask."

"Someday when you are ready, my friend. We will talk."

Something in my mind wants to know, but something also tells me I'm not ready. The question made Nobuyuki sad and may have no easy answers.

"How do we tell a place is safe?"

"Beyond what we talked about in the cart and your groundhogs?"

I nod.

"Usually, the library. Read through the history and religion section, if we make it that far. If that checks out, we stay until trouble."

"Kids are playing, that's a good sign," I say adding it to the mental list.

"Yes, so are people talking and laughing. The absence of people is usually a first warning sign."

I settle on the bench and take in the day. It's nice.

We waste an hour sitting and observing. Nothing jumps out as new. I've watched kids play long enough to not feel a direct threat. "I'm going to hit the library and research."

He's meditating. "I'll catch up with you. I'm going to check out the city. Unless you want me to walk you to the library. Your last interaction there wasn't too positive."

"Meh, I can see the stars and stripes from here. I'm adding that to my list. Check out the flag. The last one smacks my memory with brass knuckles. The Iron Cross should have been a huge hint."

"You were a little out of your mind and you bolted."

I looked at the old man. "Where's the little girl that glows red?"

The old man laughs. "You will see her soon enough. Let's talk later. I will find you." He looks at the river and takes a deep breath going from a meditative pose to standing. He walks off leaving me here with my thoughts. Oddly, everyone in the park stares at him. Usually, they glance and are done, some grab phones and take pictures.

Part of me says grab him and go. Something is up. I watch him walk out of the park and no one is following him. Maybe he's bigfoot in this world. It troubles me until a lady walks by and eyes the other side of the bench. She's got a book in hand. She almost asks if anyone is sitting there but I guess my disheveled look drives her off. She smiles at me and it hits me like a brick.

"Rebecca?" The name runs past my lips.

Her head tilts. "No, my name is Charlotte."

The sense of déjà vu is almost overpowering but I push it back down. Nobuyuki's not around to bail me out.

"I'm sorry, here have the bench." I stand and she's heavily guarding herself. "Enjoy your book."

I walk off but look back a couple of times. She watches me leave. Maybe she recognizes me too, or she's making sure I'm walking out of the area. I glance at the others at the park. There's no reaction as I go by. Nobuyuki can take care of himself.

The library is just down the street. The last world had blacked-out windows, but here they're tinted and the landscape looks different. That stupid gavel hits again and my heart is racing. I need an old Japanese man's hand to hold and look back at the park. Charlotte left. The bench is empty. I sigh and watch the library, lots of traffic going in and out. The heartbeat of a healthy library, but a wall of anxiety holds me back.

I walk in. No armed guards, no person looking me up and down and buzzing me in. Where the judge's chambers stood is the gentle wheeze of a coffee shop. A coffee shop in a library. That's cool. The smell of coffee is strong and good. I want a cup badly, but I don't know what money looks like here. As I walk off, there's a hand on my shoulder. My breath halts.

"You need a cup of coffee." It's kind eyes, framed by wrinkles and a smile. An older African American lady taps me on the shoulder and says, "Sorry, if I startled you."

I smile and laugh. "I don't have my wallet."

"You don't need your wallet here. Let Darla buy it for you."

"Is Darla someone else or you?"

She laughs and looks me in the eye. "Nope. Old Darla is me."

"Thank you, Darla."

We wait in line. The guy behind the counter is a coffee artist, but why hurry in a library? These aren't places to drop in and drop out, but to take one's time. I thank Darla excessively.

"Are you from around here?" she asks.

"No, just got in today," I say. I don't have answers to her follow-up questions.

"Where are you from?"

My mind's in overdrive. State names might not be the same, city names change, directions usually are similar. "I'm from up north. What about you?"

"Oh, Darla's been around here for a long time."

I interrupt her before she asks where I'm from up north. "What do you do here, Darla?"

She smiles at me and loves talking to people. "Oh, I've done a lot of things here, but now I work at the community center. We're having a meeting upstairs, but you know, coffee first." The barista creates foam pictures in the customer's drink. It's pretty good. He finishes and hands it off.

"What can I get for you?" the barista asks.

I look at Darla. She smiles "Get whatever you want."

"Just coffee, black."

The barista pauses for a moment. "That's it?"

"Are you sure?" Darla asks. "That's like asking this artist for a blank canvas."

"Yes, simple things."

"What would you like, ma'am?" the barista asks ignoring me from this point on.

She rattles a specialty drink but the barista takes it in stride.

"That's quite an order," I say.

"When you hit my age, you know what you like. You said you're new in town. Do you have a place to stay tonight?"

"Yes," I lie. She knows.

The barista already has my coffee done. It irritates him. He sets in on the counter with no fanfare.

"Thank you," I tell the barista. "Darla, thank you so much."

She smiles. I bet she does that a lot. She's told people some bad things in the past, but has a smile that makes the pain disappear.

"Listen." She digs for something in her pocket and withdraws a card. "Here is a list of resources. You might not need it tonight, but if you do, they'll help you out. My name's on the back if you need anything."

I take the card. The last card I had nearly killed me. I take a deep breath and look at it. Her title is Homeless Outreach Manager.

"Thank you, Darla. I'll be fine. I've got some things set up." She's heard that more than once. "Thank you for the coffee."

"You're welcome, but I realize I didn't even get your name."

"Joe." I hold my hand out. She takes it in both hands and squeezes it.

Are handshakes different in this world, or is she just kind? I don't want to repeat it to someone else and be awkward.

"You take care of yourself, Joe. You have my information if you need it."

34

"Thank you, Darla."

The barista interrupts with Darla's total. Even with her technical coffee order, the barista breezes through it.

The coffee feels warm in my hands, almost alive. I nod and tell Darla goodbye. The layout of the library seems common. I'm looking for the historical section and realize all non-fiction is upstairs.

The stairs open to a large second level. I stop on the stairs and look at the lower-level corner. No kill cylinder, but it still sends chills up my spine. There's a large local history section with pictures of old men staring at me. Lots of American flags are on display.

I look in the world history section and nothing stands out. The problem is, I never was a student of history. I couldn't tell you Egyptian dynasties, Greek wars, or Roman senators. I look for anything odd. There's always a gap of time between the fall of Rome and the Renaissance. I notice the steaming cup of coffee, sit back, and take a drink. It is a great normal coffee. Could I put a coffee maker in the trash cart? Could I make a battery to run it? Plug it into a quasar? Be a guy that hops dimensions looking for the best coffee?

I stop being silly and read again. There are tapestries of dragons and unicorns. I remember what Nobuyuki said about our first meeting. You can't walk up to a security guard and ask, "Does this world have dragons?" and not stick out like a sore thumb. I keep reading.

We get into the World Wars and find the first divergence with World War II. I try to remember high school history but pretty sure this is different. Allies beat the Nazis early on with Hitler's surrender to the Americans. The United States focuses on the Pacific War with the rest of the Allies pulling out. Then the war slows down to a crawl with heavy losses on both sides. The Manhattan Project goes forward under the name Project Guardian and finds early success with a powerful hydrogen bomb. No Fat Man and Little Boy, but an island-vaporizing juggernaut right out of my world's Cold War.

The nuclear fireball vaporized this world's Enola Gay over Tokyo, along with seven other planes over strategic targets. We honored their crews with plazas and shrines around America. There is no other mention of Japan other than its complete destruction. The eradication of the royal family led to the absence of a formal surrender.

I keep reading. There was no Cold War. The United States marched on Russia after Germany and Japan. From the end of 1955 to now there were no new wars, only skirmishes that lasted about as long as a military drill.

I'm now nervous for Nobuyuki. There were Japanese in America during World War II and we rounded them up. What the history books don't state is what we did with them. Omissions are always a "we behaved badly" part of history.

I close the book and leave it on the desk. The coffee sets steaming next to it and I wonder what to do. I grab Post World Asia and read a little deeper. The aggression toward Japan led China to become isolationist. Their conquest of the Koreas and Vietnam went quiet and diplomatically. There are books and books about what goes on beyond the jade curtain, but they are all circumstantial. I have to find Nobuyuki.

I greedily gulp down the rest of the coffee and leave the library. Outside, I'm walking back toward the statehouse. The grounds are open here. People are out on a daily stroll. I'm alone and can't find him.

A loud, raised truck drives by. Two beefy white teens in American T-shirts are on the lookout. One makes eye contact with me and nods. Chains drag behind their pickup, kicking up sparks as they drive by. American flags flap in the back. Tires screech nearby. Another truck down the street stops in the middle of the road. Teens jump out and run down the alleyway. It's on the other side of the grounds. I run.

The black truck pulls up behind them and the three teens get out. The teen I made eye contact with runs out and points down the alleyway. They rush in except for the driver. He pulls something out of the truck box, looks around, and pulls out a rifle. Our eyes lock. With a quick nod, he dashes into the alley.

I near the trucks and listen to their chatter.

"Dude, that's a Jap if I've ever seen one."

"You're living off your grandpa's memories."

"Stanley!"

There's a fight brewing and yells erupt from the alleyway. The kid with the gun aims and takes the safety off. I'm out of breath but pour everything into these last few steps and tackle the kid with the gun. I don't know what I'm doing at this point. It's all panic and adrenaline. He turned before I hit him and the rifle's wedged between us. He hits the ground hard and is dazed. I throw the gun away from the others.

"Roger?"

I look up. Three kids are down in the alley. His friends advance back at me and don't look happy. Roger tries to kick me as I roll away. I land on the rifle and his eyes go wide. There's a storm sewer not too far from where I'm at and I push the rifle into it.

"You asshole, that's like finding sasquatch." Roger points into the alley.

I stand in case he's wanting a fight. "Roger" stands up and the odds just got worse. There's a flash of white in the alley. Two boys walk out of the alley to me as the old man stands behind them. He's bloody and not happy. I square up on the two boys and Roger. From behind, the old man does a heavy roundhouse kick that makes Roger's head knock into the other kid's head like a champagne toast with three overripe cantaloupes. They're out cold.

"We need to get offworld, now. These people like the hunt."

"Go to the cart. I'll meet you there."

Nobuyuki sprints down the alley and is gone. The kids are out cold. I leave and cross the park appearing as innocent to a riot as possible. A police cruiser drives by and checks me out. They pull up to the trucks as I move a little quicker. The officers get out. One of them yells for me to stop and I haul ass. I run across the park with the police right behind me.

Charlotte probably made a good choice not to sit next to me in the park. I'm trouble. Not long after meeting her, the local peace officers try to run me down.

The Michigan Power Building lies straight ahead, but an officer is driving parallel to me as his partner chases. I run across the business park into our alley. Nobuyuki is crouched by the cart. I'm running flat out and someone's running close behind me. He's tries to radio but is out of breath.

Nobuyuki stands, opens the lid to the trash cart. The insides glow purple. The cop behind me stops. He sees

Nobuyuki and can't process it. He radios huffing air, "Control, we got Japanese in the alleyway of the Michigan Power Building." I don't stop and dive into the cart. Nobuyuki is behind me and the world goes black.

I'm trying to catch my breath in the void of space waiting for a cop to open up the top of the cart and pull us out.

"Joe, we're underway. There is nothing to worry about."

I stare at the top of the universe for the moment but feel our movement.

"This is going to be unsettling for you, but they got me."

"What's wrong?" I swim in the dark to Nobuyuki's voice.

"I got stabbed and thought it was minor, it's not. I need to heal."

"Do what you need to do. What can I do to help?"

"Not freak out. The void takes care of us." There's a sudden sleepiness to his voice. His form glows white and highlights the blood on his robes.

I move over to him and put my hand on the wound. He flinches.

"It's deep. I'm sorry." Nobuyuki glows red. The same red glow I saw from the little girl that freaked me out. "I'm sorry, Joe." The words softened like he was going to sleep.

My head feels swimmy.

"Nobuyuki?"

I touch his shoulder and get no reaction. The red glow grows more intense and I'm finding it hard to think. I push back from Nobuyuki and my head feels better.

Nobuyuki sighs, dims, and goes limp.

Lit from a flashing quasar, Nobuyuki's face elongates and robes melt away as their skin sprouts fur. Ears move from the side of their head to the top. Their teeth grow long and sharp, then the body shrinks dramatically. It's like watching a werewolf transform into a corgi. Their nose blackens and three tails emerge from the spine.

Nobuyuki is in their bright white form but their normal glow is dull. Through thick fur, I follow the blood to a slash mark on their flank. I rotate them in space wondering how to help as the red glow returns. I pull back as stupidity washes over me. The glow ebbs when I get away but the wound has a faint white glow. The edges glow brighter, until I can't look at it. When the light ebbs, I glance back. The bleeding has stopped. The wound appears smaller but is still there.

"A man and his dog on an interdimensional journey," I say.

"Call me a dog again and there will be two stab wounds in need of healing," Nobuyuki whispers.

"Are you okay?"

"Yes, I just need to rest. Leave me be for a while."

I drift away and watch a massive black hole eat a star cluster. I wish I had another cup of that coffee. Sitting on my galactic porch watching a star die. We move around the black hole riding on rivers of plasma ejecting from it. The universe shifts and soon we are elsewhere.

"Have you ever seen anything like that?" I ask to the darkness and a snore replies from the other side. No time for questions today.

I stretch out. Another galaxy comes into view. We approach the spinning arm. When we get close enough to see individual stars causing the great glow, I fall asleep.

Chapter 4

I wake from my nap refreshed. It's dark in the void and I reach out. My hand hits fur.

"Nobuyuki?"

"Hey, Joe."

I make the mistake of petting. "So, you are a werecorgi?"

Nobuyuki glows. They ebb a dull white, then glow in brilliance until I shield my eyes.

"You know I'm joking. I know you're not a corgi." The glow dimmed to where I could look.

"Would you be more comfortable if I took the old man's form? Would you stop petting me then?"

"Whatever is comfortable to you." I reach out and pet its snout. Nobuyuki nips my finger and I pull it back like I touched a hot stove.

"I am not a dog, Joe. More importantly, I'm not your dog."

"What are you?"

Nobuyuki relaxes and floats, the three tails splayed out, twitching, causing it to maintain a fixed location. There's a tension in the air and I don't know why.

"Kitsune."

Nobuyuki pronounces the consonants hard.

"Like I've said before, we've had this conversation. The last time you had a cell phone, we thought about recording it." Nobuyuki trails off.

"I had a cell phone?"

"It broke several jumps ago," Nobuyuki's voice breaks. He clears his throat. "I am a spirit. I'm old, I take multiple forms, I play a mean guitar, and love poetry."

"Multiple forms?" I ask.

"Yes, remember the little girl that scared you?"

Nobuyuki transforms into a little girl wearing a private school uniform. Her long black hair is shoulder length, she has dimples and differs completely from the old man. Nobuyuki winces and grabs her side.

"I don't want to shift too much. That wound is still there."

"Will it heal?"

"Yes, and soon. Just like everything else, it takes time."

"So, last world, Japanese annihilation. We have a different world based on WWII doing something odd."

Nobuyuki looked up. "We've shifted far. New world, new dynamics. It explains why they attacked. They didn't understand who I was."

I look back. "I watched a black hole eating. That was new."

"Where?" There is a sharpness to Nobuyuki's voice.

I look around. "I don't see it now, but it was huge and close. In that direction." I wave off into the galactic distance.

Nobuyuki passes me and peers into the void. It stares.

"You're the first of your kind to witness something like that."

"Take that, Carl Sagan. I'm Joe, the astrophysicist." I want horribly to have a last name. It's the little things that drive me crazy. I have a functional brain, then hit a wall. I know snippets of history, the names of things, the names of people. How did I forget something like Nobuyuki? Why did I have a void of recent memories but could remember the stuff I learned in high school? Why can't I remember who I am?

"You okay, Joe?" Nobuyuki asks. The glow faded back into darkness.

"Yeah, just trying to remember."

"Sometimes you will, sometimes you forget."

"Joe Sagan," I whisper.

"What's that?" Nobuyuki asks.

"Nothing. I remember I saved you from the dragon."

"You remember that?" her little voice questions it.

"No...I remember you told me."

"Joe, if you want to go out, you can. I'm going to stay and heal."

"Is it safe?"

"Is it ever?"

"No, are we always in this much danger?"

There was a sudden shift in Nobuyuki. Apologetic. "I'm sorry, it's not always bad. We've had a few worlds that were stinkers."

"I got free coffee," I say with a smile.

"Yeah? I got stabbed and beat up."

"You can stay with me or go check it out. But let's go back to our protocols."

"You mean like dragons?"

Nobuyuki laughs. "No dragons."

I hit the top of the universe and look out. The cold slaps me in the face and I almost can't breathe. It pours into the void. I close the lid and drift down.

"We always arrive at the same time?"

"Yes, but the weather may change. Spring, midmorning, usually nice weather. What did you see?"

"Cold, dark, ruins."

"Recent ruins or like older ruins?"

"Power Building's there, but it's in pieces. There are ways to get out of the alley."

"This is a doomed world. We hit them every once in a while. Don't investigate."

I push back up and look out. It's a wasteland.

Nobuyuki's under me shouting. "I wouldn't recommend without me running scout."

Arctic wind blows through the rubble. The alley is lit up like a full moon. I'm curious.

"Joe, if the sun is out, and it's a wasteland, it's a no-go. There is nothing to see here. We don't know what's out there."

"I don't know if the sun's out. Can I survive if I check it out quickly?"

"I'm still hurt. You do this, you're on your own. If you die, this might fall apart."

Something in my gut is telling me to go. I need to see something here.

"In and out."

Nobuyuki gasps in pain and frustration. I look down and the old man is there.

"Apparently, you don't listen to kids. Stay. This is a dangerous world. Let's go."

It took a lot out of Nobuyuki to shift and hurt registers on the old man's face. I look back out and exit. Nobuyuki yells, probably calling me something in another language. It's cold here like the Arctic in an endless dark winter. My jacket doesn't block the wind. I run through the rubble guided by the light of a full moon. When the wind fully hits me, it takes me to my knees.

45

This usually busy street is full of relics and old cars. The dust on them is so thick you can't tell what color they were. The most current models are from the 1970s. I crawl out and use an old Ford LTD as a windbreak. The sky is clear and cold. I look up and see the Milky Way's arm. It dims around a tiny bright moon.

Then I realize that's no moon. The sun would usually be about 40 degrees in the sky. It's replaced by what looks like a distant star in the correct place, but smaller and pale.

Something happened to the sun here and it killed everything. There are no birds, no vermin running around, no people. My core cramps and I shiver. I've stayed too long and my feet are numb, numb to the point they hurt. I'm about a minute here longer than I should be, but something tells me to wait and watch.

Trees and all plant life are gone. My eyes freeze. I blink but the wind seems to dry them out immediately. My vision doesn't break past the ruins of the buildings. The wind gusts and it drives the breath from me. I duck down and the car shields most of it, but I need to go. I violently shiver as the wind moans past. If I wait much longer, I might not move. Light snow blows down the street, but something else moves against the wind. I crawl out from the car and head back to the alley. The wind makes it difficult but I don't want to face anything that's survived this. Peeking out, it stands near the car I was just at. It looks like a semisolid shadow standing at over seven feet, its body is slim with elongated arms and legs. It touches the ground where I huddled. Its hand goes to a featureless face.

It's got my scent.

My heart stops.

Even in this gale, its blank face traces my movement and stares right at me. I bolt like a stumbling jackrabbit. My frozen legs don't respond. I stumble-run to the alleyway to the trash cart over the rubble. Perched on the alleyway wall, it's staring at me above. Lightning flashes through its insides like a nervous system as it prepares to pounce. I open the cart and dive in. The wind won't let me shut the lid, but something lands on top of it.

"Nobuyuki, we're in danger!"

My fall into the trash cart slows into space. I'm looking up. Nobuyuki in old man form with his sword drawn. The top opens to the universe as this thing looks in. I sense movement. The space between us elongates and slams shut. There's a shriek like quick frozen metal.

"Idiot," Nobuyuki yells. "You are so like a child sometimes. Next time when I say stay put, you stay put. I told you I'm not well."

I'm upside down to him and he's glaring at me. His sword's held high, casting light into space.

"What was that?"

"Did it dive in after us?"

I'm staring at him stupidly. He kicks me in the chest, not hard, but it gets my attention.

"Joe! Did he dive in after us?" Nobuyuki glows brightly and we look around in panic. We're alone.

"Space shut in around him."

"That's what I saw too, but did he make it in?"

"Can it still crawl in?"

"I don't know. This is sterile space, if we bring in something from another world, I don't know how it will act." He looks into the bleak confines and sheaths his sword. "Our safe space may no longer be safe." He grunts.

"What is it?"

"We call them Yurei. That was a doomed world. No more field trips to doomed worlds."

I'm a scolded child. The old man stares at me, backlit by a nearby galaxy, and I know his scowl. He closes his eyes and seems to darken and fade. Nobuyuki's shadow leaves and spreads out. A vibration like a pebble that disturbs the surface rings out.

"We are safe for now if it didn't follow." Nobuyuki's shoulders relax. He wants to yell.

"Have we ever seen those before?"

"I have. You have not."

"What did you call it, a Yurei? What is that?" I'm staring at him like a scared child.

"It wasn't a that. It was a they."

My head tilts. "You're a they, are you a Yurei?"

"You look at me like a stupid dog. You could have brought doom on us all." His three tails drop down from his robes.

"I didn't know."

"What you don't know would fill a library." He's so angry his form's vibrating. He reverts to his animal self.

"Calm down, Nobuyuki. You're still hurt."

The accidental transformation makes Nobuyuki flinch. The white glow begins again and there is fresh blood on the old wound.

"Idiot," he says and falls asleep. I wonder if I can use his sword, but here I am, floating in the void with a supernatural foxlike thing that wants to kick my ass.

Chapter 5

"You are upside down to the lid again. I think it's your favorite sleeping position."

I startle awake. "Nobuyuki?" I ask in the dark.

"Yes?"

"Are you okay?"

"I'm fine. How are you?" The old man's voice answers. I can't see much in the void, it's dark. As my eyes adjust the universe comes into focus. I'm upside down and it feels like waking up in a new room, while floating and not knowing which way is up.

"Are you healed?"

"So far, so good."

"Did you fully heal?"

I don't like the pause. "I'm active," Nobuyuki answers.

"Way to dodge that question."

"I'm over 300 years old. I've been bit, shot, stabbed, and almost eaten by a dragon."

"That was a life-changing event."

"There are few dragons in the multiverse. To see one is a life-changing event. To be eaten by one is a life-ending event." There is silence in the darkness. Nobuyuki is breathing in quick fits.

"Are you laughing?"

"Maybe." It's a lighter moment than we've shared recently.

"What are we doing?" I ask.

His odd breathing stops, the void suddenly seems heavier.

"Are you asking what we're doing now or in the big picture?"

"Big picture."

The old man sighed. "We've tried to figure that out. You and I are multidimensional refugees. We found each other in the dragon's den that you walked into like you were ready to order a hamburger."

"Offering a fast-food restaurant something on the secret menu," I reply.

"You were in one of your states. You were out of your mind. I think you talked to the dragon before realizing what was happening."

"Can we get back home?"

"I'm not sure where home is anymore." Nobuyuki floats in front of the universe. "I've always been a traveler. You were lost when we met with no direction back. So, like I said. Interdimensional refugees, we sometimes find places to stay and thrive, but something always goes wrong."

"I remember just a few worlds. What happened when I almost died?"

"Which time?" Nobuyuki mumbles.

"How many times has that happened?"

"In time. It takes time. When you're ready, I'll tell you." I can barely see Nobuyuki, more like a shadow in a dark room.

"Okay. You ready?"

"Yes, but let's do this with a little more regulation."

"Deal. No dead planets, no dragons."

"Here we go again."

I right myself, flailing and moving my arms around. Nobuyuki grabs my foot from the darkness and flips me with grace.

I float and feel the edge of the universe. When it opens, it's bright out. "Sunlight, that's a good sign."

"Promising."

There's life going on all around us. "We got traffic."

"Okay, so there's people."

I've seen this alleyway several times before. It looks clean, almost too clean.

"Hmmm. No laughter."

"That might be a sign. I'm going out."

A flash of fur runs up my back and pops out of the void. I should wait for Nobuyuki to return but emerge. Men in white protective suits are cleaning something down the alley with high-pressure hoses. I pop out and they both look in my direction. I walk the opposite way. The office girl is there as I pass the building's door, folders fly, and I startle her. She screams. Mike will be coming and I run. I make it to the alleyway and walk toward the park and library. Nobuyuki is on patrol and should see me. People zip around like a war zone. There are no leisure walkers. Part of me wants to go back and look in on the cleaning crew, but the hazard suits worry me.

"This one may not be safe." Nobuyuki startles me from behind a tree.

"I get that feeling."

"Then, why are you out?"

I'm in trouble again from his tone. "Wanted to see things for myself."

"Here lies Joe. Wanted to see things for himself. Did you scare the office girl?"

"Oh, yeah."

"Your Magic Eight Ball is pointing to 'no'. What are we doing?"

I look around. People are still out, life finds a way. "Do you sense immediate threat?"

"Did you see the cleaners with the protective suits?"

"Yep."

"Did you see what they were cleaning?"

I glance back to the alley. "Uh, they looked at me pretty odd. I got out of the alleyway."

"Well from up above it looked like human remains. Someone got slaughtered in the alley last night."

"Let's avoid the park and go straight to the library."

"Dangerous world, Joe. You want to research, why?"

"A feeling. Why are we ending up in these fractured areas? Maybe we can get an understanding of why we are here."

"You're doing it again. This is the quickest you've ever gone to figure it out."

"Did we get very far?"

"No, we never do."

"Why?" I ask as we pass the state building.

"We get too comfortable. The danger doesn't exist on the surface and we decide to live. With that comfort, we let our guard down, lose our wanderlust, and we fail."

"How?"

"You're not ready for that story yet."

"When will I be?" The comment takes us to the library steps.

"In time."

"When?" I ask.

Nobuyuki glares at me. "We're in a hazardous world

and you want to argue?"

He's right. Just a couple places ago, this was an extermination pit.

"What are we doing, Joe?"

I stop at the stairs landing. There are normal windows and people are walking in and out.

"It's fine."

Nobuyuki stops looking at the door.

"What is it?"

"Look at the hours of business. The closing time has a sliding scale every month, earlier to December, slightly longer after January, June was the latest."

"They close at sundown?"

"Why not set a time? It's not sundown but an hour before."

"Let's go see."

I walk up and enter the library. I know Nobuyuki isn't happy but there is a thread in all these places we have to figure out. The library appears smaller. Nobody makes eye contact and moves with too much purpose. I smell coffee. In the place of the old coffee shop in the previous world, there is a table with a simple coffee maker and some Styrofoam cups. Nobuyuki walks into the library. I wait until he's next to me.

"Free coffee."

"It's a trap." The old man scowls.

An attractive redhead is sitting in a nearby chair close to the coffee.

"It's definitely a trap," Nobuyuki mumbles.

The redhead's reading a thick book, seemingly engrossed until I approach to get coffee. Her eyes follow the page, then watches me as she turns to the next page. She stares with the most beautiful, piercing blue eyes.

She notices me watching her as I pour.

"Hello," she states.

"Hello, are you guarding the coffee? I should have asked before I poured."

She chortles. "Free coffee, free world."

"If you were a rat, it would snap your neck. Idiot!" Nobuyuki whispers behind me.

She tilts her head, looking at Nobuyuki and he senses it.

"Be careful with this one. I swear, boy. You walk brazenly into traps. With arms open."

Nobuyuki stomps off.

"Sir, would you like some coffee?" the redhead asks.

I watch him walk off. Then look at her. She's intently studying him.

"Your friend's not a fan of coffee."

I chuckle. "Ancient warrior beliefs. He's not into caffeine."

"Must be a wonderful traveling companion."

The comment stops me cold and I arch an eyebrow.

She stumbles. "I mean someone that isn't a morning person not into caffeine. Wow, how does one survive?"

"Yeah. He's not a pleasant person."

She smiles. "My name is Katherine."

"Hey, Katherine. I'm Joe." Something doesn't feel right. The hair on my neck stands at attention.

"Are you new in town?" she asks.

"Why would you ask that?"

"I've not seen you around. Welcome to Fort Wayne, Indiana."

"I am a regular."

"Oh?" It takes her by surprise. The hairs are rising

again. "I haven't seen you around."

"I recently got into research." The coffee is hot and I can't guzzle it. Nearby is a sign that says no drinks in the library. It's subtle but this spider has me in her web. I could walk off but it would be obvious.

"You can leave your coffee there and let it cool down. Go get a book. It's what the library is about." She smiles. It's easy to fall into. I take a sip. When I come back, I won't be able to drink it.

"That sounds like a plan. Thank you." I put my coffee down and she goes back into her book. She's got a plan and it has me nervous.

I walk over to the history books and scrutinize the shelves. All the books have a black sticker that says "State Approved". Another bad sign for this place. The Easy Reader World History books are first. In ancient Egypt, all the gods were reptilian and "travelers". The Dark Ages lasted until the late 1900s and the Bolshevik Revolution ended it when the people sought information and education.

World population numbers are lower. World wars created a need for history and there have been four. The last one ended in 2001 with the death of King Janek in Czechoslovakia. I stop at the picture. There is a color photograph of King Janek in regal finery. Fiery red hair and beard. Piercing blue eyes. I quickly turn the page. The Russian premier made a land grab after the war. They showed a previous meeting between the leaders. Lots of red hair among the leaders of the world. Maybe Ireland had a larger piece in the world. I look at the table of contents. Ireland became forcibly annexed by the Kingdom of Great Britain in 1960. I look up the royal family and find a sea of redheads in rule.

"This is different."

"Did you find something?" The old man's voice is behind me and it makes me jump.

"Maybe." I take the book over to a table and we sit down. "Books are all state approved," I say as I point to the black sticker on the book. "There have been four world wars and a long Dark Age. Most of the world's rulers are redheaded."

"I've known some redheads, they are passionate. No wonder they've seen wars."

"Isn't that a little racist?"

"You have one that's got some interest in you."

"Yeah, Katherine has an odd interest in you too. When you walked away, she studied you."

"Piercing eyes?"

"Yes."

"Odd moments of silence and the hairs are up on your neck?"

I look at Nobuyuki. "Yes."

"Baka!" Nobuyuki swears and slaps the table. "We are in a bad place. They've taken over here. We are in lots of danger."

"Who's taken over?"

"Remember when I said we shouldn't be in this world? You need to listen to me."

I get up and close the book. "I get it. Let's go." I look back when we hit the entrance. My cup is there alone. Katherine is gone. I've got a worse feeling than if she was there staring at me walking by. "Quickly," I say as we go out the doors. We run down the stairs, out into the public area, and near the park. The streets are empty as people rush away. Nobuyuki and I rush back to the Michigan Power Building. Katherine is near the capitol building, and she's not alone. There's a black SUV and people in tactical gear surrounding her. She points at us and they advance.

Nobuyuki yells. We split. He sprints away from me at supernatural speeds. Sirens blare behind me. An SUV chases Nobuyuki. Footsteps are closing in on me. A hand reaches for my shoulder. I dodge and get tackled hard, smacking my head on the concrete. The air is driven out of my lungs. I'm cuffed and moved down the street. I can't understand their language. It doesn't help that I'm woozy from smacking my head.

The SUV is speeding back. It screeches to a stop and a door opens. Nobuyuki is shackled and hooded. A goon covers my head with a black hood and I'm tossed in next to him. Then securely fastened and unable to move.

A rifle pokes me in the back as the SUV moves. We accelerate down streets and make quick turns. Then we descend through some type of underground garage that is either at or near the capitol building.

We stop, the doors open. Someone removes the straps, but not the hoods. I can barely see light through this. It feels hotter as we move. The air seems stagnant and the lights dim. I'm pushed through the dark. Two large doors swish open and I'm pushed into the middle of a large room, then forced down to a chair. They secure my cuffs behind me to the chair. It's uncomfortable. The hood is removed. Man, it's warm in here. Feels like the desert at sundown. Bright lights come on above me and Nobuyuki. I glance at him and he looks fine. Mad, but fine. He's going to yell at me again.

Katherine is there again. This time, no book or coffee. She's giving the rundown of how she met me in the library. She points to the old man and her voice gets weird. It's low for a female and guttural. I can't see who she is talking to in the darkness.

Their attention is on Nobuyuki, but occasionally my brain's trying to crawl out of my head and it makes the hairs stand up on my neck. When it happens, Katherine's voice clears up and I understand her.

They know about Nobuyuki and call him a dark Kitsune. I don't know what that means. They refer to me as the traveler, then the weird crawly feeling goes away and I can't understand the conversation anymore.

Katherine steps behind me and talks again. "Male, approximately forty."

Suddenly my brain feels like it's having an allergic reaction. Katherine refers to me as Subject Seven.

"Thirty-seven." I try not to throw up.

"Silence." It's a cold, serious voice that makes me not want to crack a joke.

"Identity unknown, point of origin unknown, he states he's from Fort Wayne. When I scanned him, I found odd things in his memory. There is missing time and days repeat."

The crawling in my brain intensifies as she talks. I grunt but want to scream, seeing images. The faceless creature from the last world stands above me as I jump in the trash cart. Then I panic. The crawling in my head stops and the room is full of guttural murmurs. My nose is bleeding and my head lolls forward. Now I'm properly concussed.

"I suggest protocol four on Subject Seven."

My head tingles again. It's more of a tickle than a bull trying to escape my head. I'm seeing flashes of events, but they're badly jumbled. Then I see multiple events at once.

"Rebecca?" I ask. Nobuyuki stares at me wide-eyed.

Chapter 6

I'm driving with a familiar named Rebecca. We're in a normal world. It's storming outside.

"Please stop," Nobuyuki says. "He's not ready."

Anxiety wells up like I'm watching a horror movie. Nobuyuki's little girl is in the back seat. We're on a road outside of town. Rebecca laughs. I'm focused on a conversation with her. Intently focused. I look up and there is a bend in the road. A car is coming at me in the wrong lane.

I'm thrashing, fighting the bonds. My memory is all out of alignment. The force from the hit goes through me, the spin, and lots of blood. My screams are constant and something pokes me. The blackened memory intensifies until darkness takes over my head. My panic mutes. I say Rebecca's name until the darkness encompasses all.

****

I wake up full of grief and forgotten memories. My head hurts like a hangover and I need the "hair of the dog" to take off the edge. My heart hurts for someone I can't remember. I'm strapped to a gurney and a machine makes lots of beeps. Someone wires my head and chest. It's dark, but someone's moving around in the machine's lights. My eyes can't focus. I sit up and a cold hand pushes me back down on the bed.

"Relax. You're not ready to sit up."

"Who are you?"

I still can't see her until her face is over mine. She forces an eyelid open and shines a bright light.

I grunt. She checks the other eye, shining the light and moving it away and back again. I'm blinded and can't see. She hangs the chart on the foot of the bed and sits on the bed.

"How many days do you remember?"

"I don't know." I recognize Katherine's voice and can see her in the dim light as my vision clears.

"Where was your point of origin?"

"Fort Wayne. I was born here."

"Not here."

I'm silent; my head's throbbing. There is a large thing of water that I reach for and realize that I'm shackled to the bed. "Please."

Katherine gets up and gets the water.

"Not too much."

I drink greedily before she pops the straw from my mouth.

"How far back do you remember?" Her eyes glow and I find it unsettling.

My head hurts too much to think.

"My dear, you were broken before you came here. It is not our purpose to break you further. Please, answer the question."

"I don't know. Maybe three days here, a couple of weeks there. It's hard to judge. I forget things."

She pulls back out the chart and jots notes. She's staring at me while writing.

"What are you?"

Katherine is talking to someone in that low guttural tone. She puts the clipboard on the bed and I kick it off. She picks it up and sets it in a holder. The bed clicks and unlocks. Two others join us. They're in scrubs.

"What are you doing?"

They push me out of the room. I'm out into the darkness of the building. There's movement, but I can't tell how many people are here. I look into the glowing eyes of the people moving me. We move into another room and I'm pushed under a large archway.

"Should we move him?"

"No, orders are to scan him where he is."

The bed locks in place. I'm trying to look around.

"Stay still or we will sedate and collar you."

It's a male voice. I relax on the bed. The archway moves around me laterally. It reminds me of a car wash.

A laser lights me up, placing a red grid over my body. It spins and whirs and moves down my body. As it scans, my skin tingles like a thunderstorm is overhead.

It takes a few moments to finish. I move my head up and it looks like the projection has made my body clear. I watch my heartbeat a few times and my lungs expand.

"Whoa. This is in real-time."

"Head back now."

I put my head back on the pillow. There is a bag of fluid placed on a pole near my bed.

"Don't move." The person pulls a syringe from his pocket.

Extermination memories flood my mind. The electronic beeps go into overdrive.

I look down and see the veins and arteries mapped out on my arms. He hits something and my shackles go tight. I can't move. My brain panics.

A needle pierces my skin. Quick, efficient, painless.

The warm fuzzies take over. I complain. My head's heavy and I'm speaking in slow motion. I'm dumber than normal.

"Whoa," I say to the universe as the abyss opens and swallows me whole. As I plunge into the rabbit hole, Katherine's voice echoes in my head that the Kitsune is eating my memories.

****

I wake up and gravity feels all wrong. I hang from a wall by shackles and my shoulders howl. My eyes adjust to the dim light and see Nobuyuki in fox form, curled up in a small cage.

"Well, the good news is you're healthy and apparently human," Nobuyuki says. "A typically unremarkable *Homo sapiens.* I tried to correct them and referred to you as a hairless ape, but they didn't see the humor and tased me into my original form."

"Are you okay?"

"Jittery, sore, angry. This is your fault."

"I know."

The light is dim. It's hard to see. The door slides open and three people walk in, including Katherine.

"I've never understood scientific naming. *Homo sapiens*, *Homo erectus*. You are simply a dumb ape."

The guard walks by and kicks the cage.

Nobuyuki snarls and snaps. The guard steps back and draws on the cage.

Katherine walks up to me, cool as a spring storm.

"How do you do it, traveler?"

"Remember how I don't remember or know stuff?"

Nobuyuki says something in Japanese and it makes Kathrine go white.

"Vivisection on the Kitsune. Let's see if we can figure out its shapeshifting ability before we kill it. Electricity will force it into normal form."

One of the soldiers walks off.

"I can't tell you how it works. It just does."

"Liar," Katherine snaps. Her blue eyes go paler.

"Nope, let us go and I'll show you."

Nobuyuki stares at me. I almost brought one monster in with us, but I have an idea.

"What do you need? I will have it brought here."

I sigh, like I've explained this a hundred times already.

"It has to be where it is." *I really don't know if that's true.* "I believe it's a fixed point in the space-time continuum that crosses dimensions."

I hope Nobuyuki understands what I'm trying to do.

"Where?"

"I won't tell you. You will take us there."

Katherine walks off without another word.

"We are in serious trouble, Joe."

I want to tell Nobuyuki my plan, but they will hear us.

"Is vivisection what I think it is?"

"If you're thinking it's like an autopsy on the living, then yes, it's what you are thinking."

I shudder in my chains.

"You've left dimensions on your own before. Go. This is my problem and I'll take care of it."

"If I do, we will never find each other again."

"You're so fatalistic."

Nobuyuki laughs. "I'm just smarter than you. I want to try something. You're not going to like it and I apologize. We may need a long discussion after this."

"Whatever you need to do, buddy."

"Famous last words. You sure?"

"Yes. We're both going to die if we don't do

something."

"Okay. You need to relax and make your mind as small as you can."

I look at Nobuyuki.

"Wow, that was too easy. You're going to feel like you're underwater. Go with it. Don't push to the surface."

"Okay?" Nobuyuki glows white, then shadows cross it like the moon on Halloween. Nobuyuki deeply exhales like a death rattle and its body falls into shadow. The shadowy wisps crawl toward me. It's near my fingernails and seeps in. I panic a little and hear a voice in my head, *relax*.

I close my eyes and lean back. There is pressure all around me. My ears won't pop and my head feels full. Then it settles and I'm floating like in the void. It's warm and comforting. It's like sleeping near twilight, but being hyper-aware of everything going on. When I open my eyes, the darkness is well lit.

"Whoa."

Nobuyuki's cage is empty. *Let me drive.* The guard walks back into the room with a gurney. He looks at the empty air inside the cage, reaches in, and slaps around the cage. He utters an expletive and runs off.

Katherine walks in with the guard. She's standing in the doorway with the guard and slaps the back of his head with enough force that he skids across the floor and doesn't move again.

"Where did the Kitsune go?" she snaps.

There is a menace in her confidence as she strides toward me. There is an icy confidence in a smile that shows teeth. Each step echoing in this small hell I'm in. Her motions are deliberate, unsettling, like a predator closing in for the kill. She's walking toward me.

I ready a good insult. *Stop!* That was loud in my head. My sarcasm is automatic. This is going to be hard. When I speak, I'm not doing it. My brain is interrupted when I had something important to say.

"You didn't know what that little fox thing was. It had other powers as well and is gone."

She picks up the empty cage, shakes it, and throws it across the room.

Another guard walks in and looks at the body on the floor. "Gather the patrol. We're going out with the traveler." The guard stares a little too long at the body. "Now!" Katherine snaps.

She grabs a box from the floor, opens it, and pulls out a large collar. It looks like a vicious Great Dane anti-barking collar. There is a black box on it with a cruel set of probes hanging like fangs through the collar. Katherine fits it on my neck. The probes bite and I want to say something funny. I can feel Nobuyuki staring at me, ready to hit me if I say it, but they are deep inside me and this is odd. I will stop describing now.

"Listen, fool. If you try to escape, do anything that we feel is out of the norm, this box will put you on the floor faster than anything. Do you understand?"

Four guards enter the room. They look at the body on the floor.

"Put him in full restraints."

Three guards circle me while one removes my shackles. He reaches into the box and pulls out leg irons and what seems like a ton of chains.

"Oh, I'm excited now."

Katherine pushes the guard out of the way and strikes my midsection. I vomit a little and spit it on the floor. It takes me a moment to get my breath back. *Idiot. Remain silent. If she does too much damage, I will have to exit.*

I can feel the box on my neck, humming and warming up. This thing will shock the hell out of me if it goes off. *Us.*

What happens if it does?

We will find out, I'm sure. It will break this connection.

Katherine looks at me oddly.

I felt the odd cold sensation wash up over me. My neck hair stands on end, and I quiet my thoughts. I pay too much attention to the guards putting on the shackles.

"How are you blocking me?" she asks. She knocks them out of the way and pulls a small flashlight from her pocket and looks into my eyes. I glare at her, then wince when she shines the light.

"Why are your eyes so dark, Joe?"

"Because you're pissing me off, lady."

She laughs and takes the light away. Her pupils shift from open orbs to slits. She glances at the box in her hand, then stares at me. My brain feels squeezed and I have something running down my nose. The guards finish with the arm and leg shackles. I can only shuffle. Katherine pulls a cloth from her pocket and wipes the blood from my nose. She sniffs it, then tastes it. The headache's vise-like grip relaxes.

"Carry him," Katherine commands. The guards grab me and pick me up. It's not like the romantic carry, more like they're carrying the prize pig while hogtied. We're moving quickly down a couple of halls and into a garage. They load me in the back of a large SUV, pile in, and we're moving. Katherine holds the remote, just waiting for me to say the wrong thing.

There's a cold thrill in her oddly slit eyes when she looks at the remote.

We're driving through an underground garage and there's light ahead. They didn't put a hood over my head this time. They don't think I'll get away.

We hit the daylight and rocket up a ramp. The driver stops at the street.

"Where do we go from here?"

Katherine stares at me. I'm looking down, not wanting to see her creepy eyes again.

"Go to the Michigan Power Building."

"Where?" the driver asks.

"Try New Century Plaza," Katherine says.

The driver nods, turns, and rockets down the street. We're going fast and pass the police. Their inaction lets me know these people have control here. I can barely move my arms and legs. How do we get out of this?

Wait.

Katherine looks back like she heard something.

"Now where?" the driver asks.

"Pull into that alleyway straight ahead."

The SUV swerves, almost hitting someone out on a smoke break. It's Mike.

"Those trash carts in the middle of the alley."

I look to see if the girl is by the door as we drive by and think about my ignored early warning.

"Here," I say, and the SUV stops.

Two guards get out and walk the perimeter.

"Clear," they both say and Katherine and the driver get out. They poke along in the alleyway. Katherine is barking orders. Mike watches us. When Katherine's goon takes notice, Mike runs off.

Katherine opens the door and grabs my chains. She single-handedly pulls me out of the SUV.

"Where?" Katherine asks.

I can't move but Nobuyuki makes me half nod to a trash cart. The guards moves it and I yell. "No, damn it. If it's moved it won't work."

The guards put it back. I felt it.

Not yet.

Nobuyuki walks me to the trash cart.

"You idiots moved it." I glare at the guards.

I'm tapping the cart with my hip making micro-adjustments to the cart. Moving it back and forth, side to side.

"Enough playing, Joe," Katherine says.

"I'm working on it," I yell back.

Now.

I step back and summon the portal. There is a purple glow from the trash cart. The guards step back.

Katherine steps forward and opens the lid, staring into the abyss.

"Fascinating. How does it work?"

"You step in."

She climbs into the cart. Her eyes are bright. She's made a discovery. I wait until she's half in and snap my fingers. She drops the remote on the concrete. Katherine's upper half falls onto the concrete. The lower half of her body is lost to the void.

"What?" says one of the guards. I grab the remote.

The portal reopens and I dive ungracefully into the void. It's slick and I'm covered in gore. I fall into the portal and hit something.

"Oh gross, it's Katherine's kicking lower half."

The portal snaps shut and we move. I swim up to the

surface of this possession. When my head breaks the surface of this proverbial lake, there's a little pop like the pressure just equalized in my ears. I'm back in control. Nobuyuki emerges as a black fox on a black background until they glow. I'm covered in black blood and brown fluid.

"Oh, I should have let her go deeper in."

"Yes, you got the intestines, right in half."

"Gross."

"Yes, you've polluted the house."

I kick at the lower half of the body the best I can do with the shackles on and watch it float away. Nobuyuki glides over and shifts into the old man's body. The remote's on the floor. He picks it up.

"Hey, I know I did something stupid."

He laughs and holds the remote on me. There is a click. He removes the collar, then works on the shackles and leg irons.

"I'm covered in blood and shit."

"Your girlfriend eats funky stuff."

"She was not my girlfriend." There is a pause in space. "Nobuyuki?"

"Yes."

"You were with me in the wreck?" Silence floods the void. I ask, "This is why I needed to heal before you told me?"

"Yes." It was a painful answer punctuated by the opening of a leg shackle.

"Well, the redheaded witch brought it out in my memory."

"That wasn't kind."

"No, she wasn't my favorite."

"You were dying. You had to be brought back here

and healed. It was the only way we survived." The other leg shackle popped. I can kick but can't move my arms.

We moved through the dimensions and the jerking, leggy corpse floated into nowhere.

"I don't want to talk anymore." I lean back and float. Nobuyuki continued to work on my hand shackles. I'd be comfortable, but I reek and Nobuyuki keeps moving my wrists. When the shackles release, I curl up into a ball and float in the nothingness.

Chapter 7

Nobuyuki respected my wishes and remained quiet.

"So, that's lizard people?" I interrupt the silence when I can't take it anymore.

Nobuyuki grunts a muted "Uh-huh."

"Telepathic lizard people running the government?"

"Looked like feuding tribes."

"They had frequent World Wars."

The wreck replayed again. I force memories of terminating Katherine. I am a murderer now. She would have killed us without a second thought, but I had taken a life with no warning. I wasn't sure how I felt about that.

"They have slave armies, I'm sure," Nobuyuki says, interrupting my flashback.

The shock on Katherine's face blocked out the image of the wreck. I ease into the void, but stink from dried blood and, and feel way too sticky to relax. We arrived at a new world, but I needed to clean up before the introduction.

"If Katherine was a lizard person and female, does that mean we could have introduced lizard-people eggs to the void?"

There was a long sigh in the dark. "You wait here."

When the crack of light showed into the void, the old man Nobuyuki was looking out.

"See anything?" I ask.

"No."

"No dragons or lizard folk? Are reptiles inherently evil?"

The old man flew up and out of the cart. A nearby star cluster lit up the void. All the floating blood and gross stuff is gone, along with Katherine's violently kicking lower half. Hopefully, our sixth-dimensional space is self-cleaning. I, on the other hand, need help. Nobuyuki thumps the side of the cart and slides in a bag of new clothes and wet wipes.

New T-shirt, jeans, a jacket, underwear, and shoes. Someone was feeling appreciative and philanthropic. I switch out of the old clothes and let them float while I break into the cleaning supplies. I towel off with the wet wipes until I stop feeling gross.

The nasty wet wipes go in old jeans pockets. Then I tuck everything inside and roll up the jeans. Something taps on the side of the universe.

"There is a car wash down the street. We can hose you down if you need it."

The joke cracks the old man up and he laughs a universe away. I need a shower. While putting on new jeans in zero gravity, I go into a flat spin. It takes me a moment to spin up to the outlook and I put on the shirt and crack the lid. Nobuyuki stands next to the cart, playing it cool.

I step out. "Normal world?" I ask, as I toss the murder clothes in another bin.

"Let's go see."

We walk toward the alley's end. I pass the door and the office girl doesn't react. "That's a good sign."

We hit the street. The layout is different but we spot the park.

"You still have blood in your hair."

"Noticeable?"

"Not terribly." I pull the wet wipes out of my jacket and wipe my head. Nobuyuki smacks my hand and takes the wipe, cleaning an area of my head.

"Thanks."

"We don't want people to think we're murder hobos."

Nobuyuki folds the wipe and throws it in a street trash can.

"But we are." It's bugging me but Nobuyuki seems unbothered.

"Have we done that before?"

I notice Nobuyuki looking around.

"What is it?"

"Nothing too subtle. Look around. What do you notice?"

This seemed like Fort Wayne, Indiana Lite.

"It's compacted."

"Look at the traffic."

A few cars pass. People on the street look alone and spaced out.

"Our money is good here. Let's get something to eat."

We make a beeline from the park and head downtown. The downtown holds a diner named after the owners. It changes names in every multiverse. Sal's Breakfast Stop pulls us in. Not far away a white taco truck sits out on the street. It stops me for a moment, but to laze around and drink coffee sounds amazing.

The smells in the café almost bring me to tears. A seated couple gives me odd looks when I walk in. I need a shave and a haircut. At least the clothes are clean. A waitress walks by, takes care of a couple near us, and turns to us. Both of our coffee cups are near the edge of the table, begging.

"How are you gentlemen doing today?"

The voice stops me.

"Hello, I didn't mean to scare you. Do you need a menu?" She seemed pleasant, unknowing.

In the back of my head, Rebecca screams as the car spins out of control.

"Forgive my friend. Yes, we will take menus," Nobuyuki says. "Joe will take some water too. He gets a little crazy with too much caffeine. I'll take a water as well."

She smiles. It weakens with me staring at her.

"Sorry." I look at her name tag. "Jo." It came out a little too forcefully. "You look like someone I knew."

Her million-dollar smile makes my heart skip. "I hear that a lot. I'll be back for your orders."

I'm not comprehending the menu and glance up. Nobuyuki stares at me. I hate it. He knows I recognized her and he's waiting for me to say something.

"I want steak and eggs," Nobuyuki says.

"Steak sounds good," I mumble, browsing the menu.

There is a weird silence between us when Jo comes back.

Nobuyuki's order rushes out of his mouth.

I nod and say, "Same," without looking up.

"Okay. Keep things this easy and you'll be my favorite table today."

She walks off, still scribbling.

Nobuyuki looks right through me.

"Yes. I recognize her," I say a little too loud.

"She's a familiar."

"She was in the wreck with us." A nearby group looks over at us. They go to the counter, pay their bill, and leave.

Nobuyuki's eyes go from intense to softening. "Yes, she was." Tears well up in his old eyes.

"So…you possess people?" I change the subject.

Nobuyuki wipes his eyes and is silent.

"Katherine said my eyes looked darker."

"That's usually the tell," Nobuyuki replies. "The iris looks in shadow."

"She scanned me pretty hard. I kept my thoughts at a minimum."

"It wasn't difficult for you."

"You could have always shifted and ran."

Nobuyuki's face darkens. "I'm not leaving you."

Jo interrupts the conversation. "The food's almost up."

We smile at her in unison.

"You guys from around here?"

"Yes," I say.

Nobuyuki barges in. "We are just passing through."

She smiles, nods, and walks off. There's a ring on her finger.

I sit back and try to smile, but feel terrible.

"She isn't Rebecca in every world, Joe. She's even been against us a couple of times. Those worlds suck." He takes a deep breath. "You've been a great companion."

"This isn't a breakup speech," I say.

"You are my favorite idiot."

I nod, but the wreck is still fresh in my head.

"We are all in control of our fate. Those that are ignorant of that," Nobuyuki points at me. "Suffer."

Jo brings us our steaming hot plates. The steak looks perfect with a little bit of fat and blood on the plate. Jo looks at me. "Steak sauce?"

"No, dear," Nobuyuki says with his hands together. "Joe and I are true carnivores. Nothing to hide the taste."

I stare at the food. She walks off.

"What is our fate? I mean, I'm not regular Joe here."

She's back with coffee, knowing she's interrupting. She holds a finger up. "I'm sorry, guys. You're solving the world's problems and I keep interrupting. Anything else?"

"No, we're good," I answer not looking up.

Nobuyuki smiles. "What are your thoughts on fate, dear? Do you have control, or is it already written?"

Jo laughs. "This isn't the first deep conversation to happen over late breakfast in here." She thinks for a moment. I look up at her. She has laugh lines and dark bags under her eyes. There's been a lot of stress and sadness there. "I used to think that it was already decided. But after the last decade...I hope it's not. No one is that cruel..." She trails off, halts a sob, and rushes off.

I glare at Nobuyuki.

"Don't be mad." He goes back to his steak. "We don't know the history of this place yet."

I grunt and cut into mine. I don't know the last time I ate because when I'm in the void, there is no hunger or thirst. It's steak, so I slow down the inhaling process. The first bite. I sigh. "So, what's my purpose, old man?"

"To be my entertainment," he laughs.

"Then what is your purpose?"

"A philosopher once said to ask yourself simple questions: who are you, what are you doing, where were you born? Sometimes these answers change." Nobuyuki takes a drink of coffee.

"Born?"

He ponders that. "We've had this conversation from time to time. Over breakfast or late at night watching stars. Sometimes it changes, sometimes it doesn't. It's an interesting view on philosophy. We've talked about trying to get back, but I don't know if either of us would recognize home if we saw it. Not right off. It would be interesting if your home was a dangerous world. My home world wasn't ideal. I met you after you had jumped several times and don't know where you are from."

I sit back and take a long drink of coffee. "Fort Wayne, Indiana," I blurt out. I have no idea where. This is my home in a place several universi away. It's like an apartment with the same floor plan but different paint. The deep thoughts are drawing me into a funk. I scan the room. I like this diner. Their eggs were fluffy. The steak could have been bigger, but it was still good.

Jo's back with coffee and tops off the cups. "Cleaning your plates, gentlemen. Must have been good."

I look at Jo. Her face is puffy. She had a good cry. "Food was good, service was excellent," I say. "Thank you."

She puts the bill in front of me. The dollar sign looks different. Nobuyuki takes it.

"Do we pay you or up at the register?"

"I'll take it when you are ready. No hurry. Coffee is hot and plentiful." She walks off.

It's a slow day for the diner. We're the lone inhabitants for a while, sitting back, talking fate and futures. Neither of us knows where we're going, so I guess that's what brings the suffering. Jo keeps bringing us coffee and the occasional water. We're full. Nobuyuki pulls out some foreign-looking money and places it on the bill.

Jo approaches. "If you guys go, what will I do for the rest of the day?"

She laughs, we laugh, it's the exchange of money and Nobuyuki says to keep the change.

"Are you sure?" Jo eyes him.

Nobuyuki smiles. "Chase your fate, dear."

I don't know how much he put on the table. She pauses a moment like she wants to say something, then leaves without another word.

We leave. I'm walking down the street. "How much did you tip her?"

Nobuyuki smiles. "Enough for a small adventure but not enough for the grand adventure."

"How did you get the money?"

"Some days, Joe. Too many questions." He walks in front of me a little faster.

We walk down the main street. There's a new city square with a lot of food trucks. Maybe that's why the afternoon business was slow. Fusion foods, meat on a stick, and a taco truck. It smells wonderful and confusing all at once.

There's a young Mexican man working at Sancho Tom's Taco Truck. The truck is simply white taco truck style, but something is familiar. He sees us and gives the nod. "Hey, Joe. Want some food?"

I stare at him, he looks familiar. "How does he know me?"

Nobuyuki answers, "Thanks. We just ate."

"No problemo. Glad to see you're doing well,

travelers. See you around."

"He's another traveler we've run into before."

I remember the location.

Nobuyuki stops and looks me in the eyes. "He's a big-time problem. Don't ever talk to him."

"Does he know how to travel?" I look at Sancho Tom in the distance. "Maybe this is what we need to get home."

"No. Big no." Nobuyuki grabs my arm and pulls me down the street like a child. "I've seen him before and always in a troubled world. That might be our sign to flee."

I look at the library.

"We ignored the signs last time. Do you want to meet another lizard person?" Nobuyuki asks.

"Is he a lizard person?"

"No, he's something completely different. If I had a guess, he's like some sort of chaos god."

"God of Taco Trucks. I bet his food is amazing."

Nobuyuki shakes his head. "Your survivability is sprinting to zero and you just ate."

"Should we hit the library or park?"

"Yes. Zero." Nobuyuki stops pulling me. "Park. I'm not going to the library here."

"So, can your people possess?" I ask again.

"It's something we don't discuss," Nobuyuki finally says.

"What are you?"

His head's down, not looking forward. I try to remember the name Katherine called him.

"I tire of this form," he finally says. We enter the park and there isn't anyone around. Nobuyuki passes behind a tree. Where an old Japanese man walked behind the tree, a young Japanese schoolgirl steps out.

She walks over to the swings, gets on, and kicks her legs. I stare a little too long. This is the girl who held my head when my memories went to mush. This is Nobuyuki and I hit a nerve with my questions.

There's a nice comfortable bench not too far away and I sit down, looking at the smaller city around me. Architecture is different. Nobuyuki says the money was different. We should be at the library trying to figure it all out, but so far libraries and buildings have been dangerous. People arrive and children play. No one talks to Nobuyuki or me, and watching a kid swing by themselves gets lonely after a while.

I sit on the swing next to her. "Do we need to go?"

"I don't know. The last few worlds took a lot out of me and I need to rest. That was more power than I used in some time healing myself." She shakes her head, deep in thought. "It's not a good sign seeing the Taco God. Neither is this constant jumping multiverses. We need to stay a while. Too many different harmonies in these worlds cause our bodies to get confused."

I must have looked confused.

"Each world has its own frequency," she says as she kicks higher. "We need to attune to one harmony or it can make us very sick. I think we have a couple more jumps in us, but we will start seeing issues soon. It feels like your body's freezing while it's getting spaghettified," Nobuyuki says.

"Doesn't sound fun."

"At some point," Nobuyuki continues. "We need to figure out what's going on. We've been chased enough here recently and I'm down for a fun day."

She puts her feet down, kicking out streams of sand.

There is a small merry-go-round and she runs for it, spins, and hops on. She moves to the center, lies down, and watches the sky. I go back to the bench and let Nobuyuki have her time.

Another hour goes by and I'm feeling antsy. I want to figure out what's going on here before it gets dark. I go tell Nobuyuki who is running around a large piece of equipment. An earlier kid says it was a pirate ship, but no amount of squinting makes it look like it.

"I'm hitting the library. Do you want to go?"

"No. You don't learn, idiot." She doesn't look at me. We need our own space for a while.

"Okay, don't get me in trouble for leaving a little kid at the park by themselves."

"You know I'm several times older than you."

"Yeah," I trail off. "I know." I get up and walk toward the library.

The streets are a little busier but not by much. Near the library is a science center with my favorite banner up, Free Wednesdays. I head in. Unless this world changes the days of the week, and it's happened before, I don't have to pay.

I look at the whirly gigs and animatronics in the front. Drones move on one side and a small T-Rex roars at me from the corner. The clerk looks up and waves me in. He asks for my zip code, and I say three blocks from here. He shrugs, puts something in the computer and says to go in. Lots of mechanizations are in the lobby, some complex, and I keep walking. I go through the hall that talks about the geology of Fort Wayne. The river has a little different zig-zag pattern than what I'm used to. They have erosion simulators here. I go upstairs and find a small room. It has a sphere in the center of it displaying the past year's weather. It shows some big hurricanes and major storms in the Midwest. Then it talks about world temperature. Cooler than normal and falling. That's interesting, global warming is a side effect of almost every new world.

There is a hall that exits from this room and I follow it. Long walls about the history of epidemiology. I'm walking through, not really paying attention until a slide stops me cold. Over thirty years ago a virus hit mankind. It ravaged more than the black plague and two world wars put together.

I go back a bit and research the timeline. Civil war, World War I and the Spanish Flu, World War II, Korea, Vietnam, Middle East War and MERS. After the fall of Iraq and Iran, the armed forces left and brought back a virus to their homes. It had a 30% fatality rate. The hardest hit were coastal areas, but the Midwest took a big hit the year after it arrived. The virus attacked the lungs and was relentless.

There's a photo of a local graveyard. It's huge. The size of a megamall and it's a city of the silent. I look at the end of the presentation hall. The virus went through its stages. It had a brief resurgence three years ago. The presentation ends with "It could happen again." It exits into a large room with a huge window overlooking the river.

A man walks past me and coughs. I react to it like a vampire sensing garlic. This is a plague world.

I go to the window. This is the back area of Lawton Park. The place that Nobuyuki is playing at is part of a memorial. I look down and there is a visual map to where the plague pits are in the memorial, divided by months, during the worst part of the disease, weeks.

I don't want to be here anymore and leave the Science Central Museum. When I get to the park, my bench is uninhabited. I need to go to find Nobuyuki.

It's getting a little later as the white taco truck moves up the street. He edges over into the parking lot. A horn plays the first couple of notes of "La Cucaracha" but the notes sound off, the last horn fails and sounds like a bad goose call. It's also probably one of the worst theme songs for a traveling restaurant. Sancho Tom jumps out and puts his banners on display. He already has a crowd starting to form. I look around and don't see Nobuyuki.

I walk over. Sancho Tom's Taco Truck has branding. There is a background of old Mexico painted in brown with a rainbow overhead raining tacos. That's memorable.

"That's what happens when you ask kids to design your taco truck." He's looking at me from the back window.

"Sancho Tom?" I ask.

"That's me, buddy." He laughs. "Hungry?"

"A little." I'm fishing for money from this world. What I have doesn't look right.

"It happens." He's a chipper one with a million-dollar smile. "Hey, come around."

There's a group of people waiting on the food he's preparing. I wait and read the story of Sancho Tom's. Immigrant grandparents who used to cook on the streets of Mexico City. There's a picture of a young boy stirring a pot with his grandmother. Then he's cleaning tables at his parents' restaurant in Arizona. He's got several culinary awards from college. Finally, a clean white truck with him proudly holding money. He's traveled the US and ended up being one of the hottest food trucks in

Fort Wayne.

Groups of people get their food and look happy. He's got a little card table with tiny plastic cups with what I guess are different salsas. The crowd hits the table like a whale going after plankton. They pass, inhale, and the little salsas are all gone except for a few lone spicy survivors.

"And that's the story of Sancho Tom's." Tom stands there with a Styrofoam container looking at the destruction of the salsa table. He hands it to me and I put my hands up.

"I'm sorry, I don't have the correct cash."

"Oh, let me see."

I pull one of the odd bills out and he looks at it and laughs.

"Ah, from out of town." Tom smiles. "But you said the magic words, I'm hungry. Come on now, don't look at it like it's poison. It's some of the best street tacos in this part of the United States."

He's a showman and a salesman. I like the guy. Especially when he waves off the bills and hands me the container.

I take the Styrofoam container and open it, finding four street tacos. They're begging to be eaten. Pork meat, some sort of slaw, and a drizzle of salsa. Simple, and simply delicious. I inhale one.

"Thank you."

"You're welcome, buddy. How have you been?"

"I'm doing okay, especially with free tacos."

"Every day with free tacos is a good day." He sighs. "We've met before and you don't remember me."

"I doubt it. I've been to lots of places."

"So have I…lots of places."

"My name is Joe." I absent-mindedly stick out my hand.

"I know." Tom laughs, takes off his plastic gloves, and shakes my hand.

Oddly, I expected something when shaking his hand. A lightning strike, memory, or maybe a chorus of angels.

"No one shakes hands here. You are from a different place." That wry smile comes up again.

"Joe!" Nobuyuki shouts from across the park. The old man is sprinting toward us.

"Yep, and there is your companion."

We watch him run. It always amazes me watching Nobuyuki run in his old man form. He stands next to me, giving a dire warning and I think it's cool he's not out of breath.

He eyes Sancho Tom suspiciously.

"Hey there." Tom puts his hand out, Nobuyuki nods in his direction.

"I know who you are." Nobuyuki ignores his hand and looks at my food. He slaps it from my hand.

"Hey," I whine.

"Did you eat anything?"

"I had a street taco. It was delicious."

"Simple idiot. Simple…stupid idiot. *Baka!* What did I tell you?" Nobuyuki looks like he's about to smack me and pulls me away. "We need to move."

"Your friend looks like he wants to talk to you, Joe. I'll see you around," Tom says.

"Thanks for the tacos." I turn to wave and almost lose balance as Nobuyuki yanks my arm.

"You got one. You'll be back for more."

Nobuyuki stares hard at Tom. "Don't talk to him

again."

I pick up the container and throw it in the trash.

"Sorry, Tom," I say as Nobuyuki almost wrenches my arm from the socket.

"And you're eating tacos in a plague world?" Nobuyuki glares at me. "What did I tell you about him?"

"You said don't." I want to argue like a five-year-old that's been denied McDonald's, but still passes by it. "He pulled up, and I wanted to see what it was."

"Do you know mythology, idiot? Maybe the story of Persephone?"

"No."

"No, of course you don't." Nobuyuki grunts. "There is no free food and stay away. That's the myth."

"We don't know what we're dealing with."

I look back. We're not too far from the park. "Are we in danger?"

"I think we're fine as long as we're away from people."

"I want to go back and look at something." We spin around and head down a mostly empty street toward the park. A couple of blocks in the business section or what used to be the business section. We pass an empty store with a faded gaming system poster in the window. There are several empty stores here. By the looks of them, they've been empty for several years. We make a couple of blocks and I cut to the west. There's a small footbridge over the river and enter a huge cemetery. This was the addition to the park. The old plague pits I saw from the Science Center.

There is a viewing area and Jo from the diner stands, staring at a certain area.

"We can't put roots down here," Nobuyuki says

with a mark of sadness in his voice.

"I think we could get happy and fat. The food is good."

"It's all comfort food and there is a reason. You have generations in mourning."

"Do you think it will happen again?"

"Yes," Nobuyuki says. "And soon."

There is a long pause. Jo looks up and sees us watching. She looks at us for a moment, then goes back to her morbid watch.

"Come on. This world is not for us." Nobuyuki grabs my shoulder and we wander back to the Michigan Power Center. Most of it is in silence. "We've had enough time here."

We hit the alley. The security guard and office girl are outside on a smoke break. We walk past and they don't even notice us. The office girl mentions the outbreak overseas. Their silence after saying that broadcasts their fear.

The top of the trash cart is glowing purple. I open and Nobuyuki jumps right in with the grace of a master. I dive in and feel the topper smack my feet. We're in the void. It's absent of smell and I'm glad. Not sure what happened to the lizard entrails, but I'm fine with it.

I'm upside down as Nobuyuki shifts into his fox form and soon glows bright white. "I want to heal you too, just in case."

He goes into meditation and glows brighter. I see no shadow but look away. I float in the void with a belly full of food from doomed people. My mind goes back to Jo. I see Rebecca and hear the squealing of tires and her scream.

"Another place, another time," I whisper as the universe goes into motion.

Chapter 8

I wake up and a red glow is surrounding me. My head is in the old man's lap and he's doing the slow murmur of his Buddhist meditation. The inflections rise and it's almost over. I close my eyes and float. The red glow permeates my eyelids.

Nobuyuki closes and the red glow fades.

"Am I healthy?"

"Brain damaged, but otherwise okay."

I open my eyes and look at Nobuyuki. "Is that a joke?"

"No, you are."

My head feels fuzzy. "What was the last world?"

Nobuyuki stares at me. A nearby trinary cluster illuminates his eyes in the darkness.

"Plague world."

I try to think and it comes back to me. I remember the taco truck.

"Who was that guy?"

"He's dangerous. That's what you need to remember. He's not human and recognizes us which makes him dangerous."

"Or a salesman."

There is a pause in the conversation.

"The Devil from your mythology was a salesman too. Million-dollar smile."

"So, what did you see when you looked at him?"

90

"He glows. I've only seen it in very powerful people before. Like walking deities."

"Like a Taco God." I know I'm staring at him like a child.

Nobuyuki sighs. "The ones that walk among humans, yes. My people can see the celestial energies."

"Do I glow?"

"Just like in life, you are dim."

"Oh." I'm a little deflated. I am not a normal human being. Nobuyuki must have sensed it.

"When you summon the void, you glow briefly. It doesn't last long and then it transfers to the trash cart. It's a different type. Your power comes from something else. You tear Spacetime."

"It starts with me?"

"Oddly enough, yes."

"Do I need the trash cart?"

Nobuyuki shrugs. "We've never tried otherwise. It would be handy while being chased by monsters or idiots."

"Nature is never that easy," I say.

"But Nature will always find a way."

There's a hole in my recent memory. "What did we do in the last world?"

"We split up. I think you went to a science place and learned about the plague. I found some articles in the library warning that it was happening again overseas, so we left."

We pass a nebula, the glowing plasma is gorgeous. I stretch out and knock into Nobuyuki.

"Sorry."

"What are you thinking about, Joe?"

"I feel like I'm forgetting something important."

"I wasn't with you very long. I'm sorry. It might be a reaction from some of your previous trauma."

I still feel full. There is a sense that the forgotten moments revolve around food, but there isn't much point in asking Nobuyuki what he didn't see. I float in the void and Nobuyuki moves away. I try to look in the shadow of space and can barely see him there. It seems like we've traveled for a while.

"Seems to be a distance between worlds."

"We need to take it easy when we go out." Nobuyuki's voice is tinny. "Don't be cavalier. When we travel this far something odd is going on."

"Great. Can't wait. Looks like we got some time to talk."

We pass a star close. It lights us up. I float in the warmth and take a moment to soak it up. Then I spin around and look at Nobuyuki. I expected to see a white fox, but sitting there is something different. Nobuyuki appears like a shadow. There are stars within him. I look at him oddly and quickly the white glowing fur returns.

"I thought that was your normal form. Which is it?"

"I'm absorbing the sunlight. When I fill up, the glow returns."

"Are you weakened when you're dark?"

"I healed us both. It takes a lot of energy but we can't get sick and take it to another world. That along with all the previous energy I've expelled, I need to rest. I've still got a little healing going on as well. Stop being so curious." I hear the disgust in their voice.

"Every world has something different. This may have been something I knew before, but then I forgot everything. Come on, buddy. You're my traveling companion. I should know what I'm traveling with."

There is a brief laugh. Then it looks at me. The white glowing form ebbs and disappears. The small stars return constantly moving through its body. Then even the stars seem to fall. Within the void is palatable darkness. Even in the full sunlight, I'm cold. The light ebbs and rushes into Nobuyuki. Their silhouette glows, but Nobuyuki looks made from the stuff of black holes. Light forms a halo around their form. My mind begs no, but I reach out and touch it.

I touch the fur and leave a brush of light. "That's cool."

"You had a bad reaction last time I showed you. I was injured and couldn't maintain my normal form. It frightened you."

I pet Nobuyuki knowing I'll be bit. It takes me back to a childhood memory of an old black Labrador. An old memory surfaces. I don't remember the house and the room, but I remember the dog. In the dark, I'd pet her in the winter and see the glow of blue sparks jump through her dry fur.

"Don't pet me. I'm not your dog," Nobuyuki interrupts.

"Sorry, childhood memory. Can you read my mind?"

"No, but I can tell when you're thinking about your old dog. You've told me hundreds of times. You're easy to read."

I take my hand back. The local stars move off and we lose light. The glowing outline of Nobuyuki's fur descends into absolute darkness. Their figure looks like a hole in space.

Nobuyuki's eyes reflect in an unnerving red, like twin furnaces trying to heat the hellscape.

"Had enough?" Nobuyuki asks.

"Takes some getting used to, but I bet I did too."

There is silence in the void, but the deepest blackest patch fades away. The stars swarm in the fox form once again, flying like distorted fireflies in a jar. I float, try to sleep, Nobuyuki is in no mood for conversation. There are questions I want to ask, but fear they will sour their already hot mood.

I wonder where Katherine's legs floated off to?

Chapter 9

It's an odd feeling claustrophobic in the vastness of space, maybe like agoraphobic with the fear of open spaces. Sometimes the sixth-dimensional place feels like a three hundred-square-foot unfurnished glass house. I can see to infinity, but the wall is right there.

I float in the deep end of eternity with nothing around me watching the universe move. My arms and legs hurt from lying still and floating. I've been asleep for a while.

"I want a science-fiction world with flying cars." A cool Buck Rogers moment.

"We've slowed down," Nobuyuki says.

The celestial movement stops and I reorient myself to the top and peek out in this world. It's cold, lots of snow on the ground, humanity hasn't been here in a while.

"Dead world," I comment as I look out. "This could be the previous place with the fuzzy people."

Nobuyuki has taken the little girl form and crawls up next to me. "I didn't see it, I was injured."

There is a lot of snow, I look out enough to see if there are tracks in it, but it looks untouched.

I open the top of the trash cart and see snow slide off around me. The sun glares upon us with a tiny, undead eye. The wind howls outside, but the alley wall protects us.

"This is exactly how the other world looked."

"Whistle if anything approaches."

Nobuyuki shifts back to the fox form and launches up the wall. They lose traction in the snow and ice frantically trying to climb a little higher. Then a little farther up, a hard gust of wind knocks them down. I watch in horror as they plummet, but Nobuyuki simply stretches out, tails angling for control, and flies across the alleyway out into the open. It's high enough that they landed on one of the nearby building rooftops.

I step out. The snow is shin high. The Michigan Power Building is a charred, broken tooth, six-story ruin. Ice formed on the side of the building that made Nobuyuki lose its grip. It's going to be a hard walk. In this world, there is no Mike the guard, no office girl, no taco trucks. The last memory feels wrong. Taco truck, I try to remember but I have no memory other than a hunger for tacos. I stop as the memory hits me, Sancho Tom, peace, love, and Sancho Tom's.

There are no vehicles other than total scrap. Smashed or burned parts appear here and there in the snow. I want to explore further. It would be a long, cold walk in foul weather to an end that would have no payoff. There are no intact buildings and even fewer places to hide. The wind is wailing and frostbite is becoming a real possibility. I weigh my very limited options and see no outcomes available. Nobuyuki is on part of the alleyway wall. I trudge back, my legs and feet are frozen and hard to move.

Nobuyuki jumps down closer to my approach. We're both shivering and not able to tolerate the cold. I open the lid to the void. Nobuyuki dives in and I climb in. Off in the wind, I hear "La Cucaracha".

"Get in and shut the lid," Nobuyuki yells from below. It must be a trick of the wind. I listen. "Now, Joe! Or you'll freeze to death." The low goose note echoes off the ruins as I dive in.

Chapter 10

The normality of the void hurts: basic pressure, no wind, and comfortable temperatures. My legs and feet wake up. It feels like they're boiling in water. Nobuyuki makes me take my shoes and pants off. They're difficult to remove. Nobuyuki glows white and my feet are red and swollen. I touch them and the skin is firm and hurts.

"You would have lost your legs if you stayed out much longer."

My feet ebb to a dull roar. "Sancho Tom was out there."

Nobuyuki hesitates. "That's impossible. I saw no human presence there."

"Did you see the mist people?"

The fox shifts to the old man. "There was nothing. That was a dead planet."

He reaches out and touches my legs. That red glow flares from his hands and sneaks up my legs. The burning slows and Nobuyuki murmurs a prayer.

We're both taking unnecessary risks and getting injured and need to find a normal world. The void is in motion. We take a long drive around the cosmos and pull around a solar system that looks a lot like ours. We move closer to the pale sickly sun and plasma flares off the back side.

"Nobuyuki, look."

There's a void rotating near the sun. A small hole

with a border brighter than the blue star. It's pulling off plasma, but the center is soul-crushing black. I almost feel we're pulled into it. As Nobuyuki's red glow disappears, the pain flows back in. Not terrible, but not comfortable either.

"Did you say the sun had a similar sickness on the other frozen world?"

"I've seen other black holes, but this is the first affecting our sun."

Nobuyuki stares for a moment, grunts, and goes back to murmuring. For a moment, I can tell the words are different from the healing mantra I've heard over and over. He goes into a long guttural moan at the end. It echoes across the void. Then a sound like a demonic blue whale calls back sending shivers up my spine.

Nobuyuki stares off at the black hole. Then touches my leg and murmurs the healing prayer again. I'm staring wide-eyed at the event horizon. That answer back is still rattling around in my head.

"What?" I ask.

"Don't. Not now," Nobuyuki responds and goes back to prayers.

I watch the tiny black speck fold away as the universe shifts. We're already elsewhere. Dimensions away. I want to ask questions. Nobuyuki just talked to a solar system monster but isn't in the mood for additional conversation. I just hope the next world doesn't kill us.

It's a long ride back. Nobuyuki slouches when done with the healing and floats to the side of the void. I barely see him as he meditates, but the room flares and Nobuyuki's fox form burns white for a while. The glow dissipates and we're in the dark again. The stars within Nobuyuki move in opposition to what's outside. Its own galaxy reflected and contained with twin points of hellfire watching me.

Chapter 11

Sleep is easy here.

"Joe," Nobuyuki calls my name and I snap awake. "We've been stopped for a while."

"Give me a minute." I'm shaking out cobwebs.

I float to the top and touch the boundary of the void. Breaking it brings the sounds of birds, cars, and people. A train hollers in the distance.

"Sounds good." I peek out. It's a normal alleyway and our buildings look good. The sun shines overhead with no dragons, lizard people, or mist men threatening…yet.

"Let me wake up a little," I say.

Nobuyuki's fox form runs up behind me and out. I find my pants floating in the void. They're defrosted and slightly damp. I put them on. I hate damp shoes, but they will have to do.

Nobuyuki returns and taps the lid.

"Are we good?" I ask.

"We're safe," says the tinny voice outside the cart. I open the lid and ungracefully exit. Nobuyuki is standing next to me in little girl form.

The office girl safely ignores us as we walk by. On the street, the city seems full and busy.

"Park first?" I ask.

"Yes," the answer is distant.

It's an odd instinct, but I put my hand out. "You

okay, kid?"

Nobuyuki takes my hand. We walk down the street to the park in a world we don't know. It's bigger than normal. From the park, a boat launches into the river. There is a newly updated playground. Instead of sand, there is a soft material that lines the play area. Nobuyuki lets my hand go and walks to the swings. I follow and push her, waiting for her to snap and tell me she can do it, but there is no complaint. She makes it to altitude and I'm pushing less and less. I find my typical bench occupied by a mom and a large bag. Her kids are playing around the mock pirate ship. She sees me look at the bench and clears off her bags.

"There's room," she says. I walk over and sit. The sun feels fantastic in that mid-spring warmness that just shies away below hot.

"Thank you," I say as I sit down. We watch our kids in a protective silence. "This day is gorgeous."

"Might rain later, but I agree," she adds.

We sit in the odd silence a little longer. "Sun feels like it's back for the year. I can't wait for summer."

"How old is yours?" she asks. I silently laugh and want to say a couple hundred years old, but don't want to scare her off. Eight seems about right. "Eight." There is an accidental inflection.

"Where does she go to school?"

Ah, the name game. Too dangerous to use the old Fort Wayne names because I don't know this world, its history, or its places.

"I'm homeschooling. We just got into the area."

"Oh, my two go to Lincoln Elementary."

"Good school?" I ask, not needing an answer.

"Well, the fourth-grader really loves his teacher, but

the second-grader needs a harder classroom. He's bored."

"That's why I homeschool." I lie. "This girl's so smart. She's got the wisdom of an old man in that little body. She just absorbs everything."

An alarm goes off on her phone. "Come on, boys." They groan and want to be here all day.

"Got to get them back, just wanted to treat them today." She smiles, gathers her stuff, and gets the kids.

Nobuyuki and I have the park to ourselves. On the swing, she's hitting the high altitude. She's working through something.

I watch the lady take her two boys and walk off. Then go sit next to Nobuyuki and swing. Hey, everyone needs to jump in a swing every so often.

"Are you okay?" I ask as she flies by.

"I'm fine." It's the rushed answer that tells me it's a lie. Something is upsetting her.

We swing in silence, except for the chain and hanger groans.

I slow down and stop. Nobuyuki keeps going. Looking around, planes are in the sky, cars are driving, and people are walking. There is no heavy feel of an authoritarian regime. I think we found a peaceful world. My ennui is getting the best of me.

I stand up from the swing.

"This time, go to the library so I'm not looking everywhere for you," she shouts.

"I will."

No one is around and I'm safe leaving the ancient eight-year-old to play in the park. I wander down to the street and see the library off in the distance. I approach and check out the flag. There are fifty stars and thirteen stripes. I walk into the library and find it on the bigger side of what I've seen before. No redhead huddled in the corner with intense eyes. Check. There is a coffee shop, but until I figure out money, I won't chance it. There are volumes of history books, and I find one good meaty tome. Flipping through it, everything feels in place.

I close the book and put it away. The religion section draws me in and I move into folklore. There is a book on Japanese spirits that I pull and browse. Lots of angry ghosts, a possible explanation of the mist people, but I need more information. There's a page with an illustrated two-tailed fox. I stop and read about the kitsune. There is so much on this page that clicks and makes sense. The kitsune are shapeshifters, have unnatural abilities, phase shifting, and flight. I turn the page and find the Nogitsune. The picture stops me. A dark fox with glowing red eyes, another picture has it turning into smoke and drifting into a person's hands. The chapter begins with a warning. If humans are tricked, tormented, or possessed by a kitsune, it is caused by a nogitsune. They are creatures of immense wickedness. A footnote calls out the mazoku, and states "A supernatural being intent on evil, against the will of the tribe of gods and mankind."

A chill runs up my spine and doesn't go away. Someone watches me as I shut the book. I slip it on the shelf and remember the name of the book.

Nobuyuki watches from the other end of the library. I wave and walk over like nothing bothers me. "We're in a safe place."

"I think so, too," she answers, as her stare goes out the window.

"Do you want to stay here or venture out?" I ask.

"Let's go."

We walk out of the library and onto Main Street. We pass a barber and Nobuyuki is staring at me. "Let's get you cleaned up."

"We don't have money."

"Yeah, we do."

Better not to ask where this came from. We walk into the barber. An older, bald, black man with a short white beard is working on a customer.

"Take a seat and I'll be with you soon."

The customer appears well-groomed, a business type coming in to get a haircut before running off to seal a billion-dollar deal.

They're discussing stocks and current markets. The barber is in clean-up mode.

"All right, see you in a month." The barber shakes the customer's hand and takes his cash, walking him out of the shop. He returns, cleans the last customer's remnants, and eyes us.

"The girl's got pretty hair, but buddy, you need some help."

I walk over and sit in the chair. He swings the smock over me and looks at Nobuyuki.

"How human do you want it?"

Nobuyuki giggles. She puts her finger to her chin like she's doing deep math. "Clean him up like the last guy."

"Don't I get a say in this?" I ask.

"You get your say, but kids make the ultimate decisions." He gestures and Nobuyuki nods. The barber turns to me with a wicked grin. Then turns to Nobuyuki and asks, "There is a dog groomer up the street."

"You'll do a fine job on this dog," Nobuyuki replies.

I've heard the lilting giggle before and the barber is falling for her grift.

He spins me around and looks me in the eye. "I got a plan, but she's asking for the full works. Are you good for this?"

I sigh. "We're good." I nod to him. "But keep the beard."

He washes my hair, complaining about something gummy. He partially dries it, then under the trimmer's hum, goes to work. Hair is falling around me like heavy snow. My hair takes shape. It's been a while. He goes through a checklist of conversation starters, asking if I follow football, baseball, boxing, or hockey. I quickly answer "no" to each prompt. He turns to Nobuyuki. "He's a great talker. One of the last orators. You should get him out more. We got a pretty good minor league baseball team here."

"Baseball?" Nobuyuki practically squeals.

"What do you have going on tonight?" He walks over to Nobuyuki.

I sneak a glance in the mirror. The person looking back at me is someone I don't know.

"Dad?" Nobuyuki says. It throws me, as I still try to figure out this mirror person.

"No. Nothing tonight, honey," I mutter.

He walks back to his desk and fishes something out of his drawer. Two tickets. "I'm a seasoned pass owner, but ended up with a hot date tonight. You want them?"

Nobuyuki's eyes light up. "Oh, baseball. Can we?"

"Sure," I say.

The old man walks over and gives Nobuyuki the tickets. She shakes his hand. He smiles and walks back to me. "See. Next time we can have a good conversation about sports."

"Thank you."

"You are welcome, sir." He works a little more on the hair, then takes a deep breath. "Now for this beard. Lift your chin and don't worry, I ain't no Barber of Saville."

I must look clueless, because in his next breath, the barber sings.

"Do you always talk about homicide when you cut near someone's throat?" I ask.

"Only to my new favorite customers." He winks at Nobuyuki and breaks into another odd song. I glance over at her and she's playing the little girl part too well. A smile ear-to-ear, an occasional giggle on the high notes the barber hits, and an over-excited clap.

A small bush releases from my face. I have cheeks and a chin. The barber sets the chair back up into the fully upright position. Something in the back of my memory says not to look, but I ignore it and look in the mirror. A clean haircut and trimmed beard unleash memories. This is the old me.

Nobuyuki and the barber are talking. She pays him, but I'm drowning. I'm trying to break the surface, but keep getting pulled deeper. I'm about ready to panic. Nobuyuki reaches up and takes my hand.

"Dad? You okay?"

I stare at her, waiting for the weight of water to crush me and find a fair-weather day. I look in the mirror, trying my hardest to get any shred of memory. The only memory I get is Rebecca screaming.

"Dad...Joe?"

Nobuyuki shakes my arm.

"Sorry, guess it's been a while since I looked this

good," I finally reply.

The barber holds out his hand. "My name's Marvin. It's good to meet you, Joe. Use those tickets tonight and don't let them go to waste. Okay?"

"Thank you, again, Marvin," I say, shaking his hand.

Nobuyuki yanks on my hand. "I paid him. Let's go wander around before the game."

"You two take good care." Marvin waves as we leave.

"He was nice," Nobuyuki says. We walk downtown for a while and decide to get some hotdogs at the game. "What happened in there?" Nobuyuki asks.

I want to talk about the memories and ask how she stopped it. It feels like I avoided death and ended up with a sucker and a warm towel.

I'm thinking of how to phrase it and decide to go with my bypass question.

"Should I be worried that you always get money in these places?" I ask.

"Nope. What's the saying? 'Don't look a gift horse in the mouth.' "

We walk in silence. The stadium isn't too far away. We pass another park and lots of open green spaces. The stadium towers over the normal buildings. It's about an hour before the game. We pass a Farmer's Market and look around. I need to relax. Sometimes, it feels impossible. People don't stare at me, because now I'm finally normal.

"You pass for a human with a haircut," Nobuyuki replies.

Did I say that out loud?

"Say what out loud?" Nobuyuki arches an eyebrow as a stream of people gather for the game. She ignores the comment and pulls me into a business. She's a giddy little kid in a store of pop culture. I couldn't see Nobuyuki's old man getting excited and holding up a lunch box. The thought makes me smile. Nobuyuki has a lot of personalities and I haven't seen them all yet. Something tells me I haven't seen all her forms either.

Nobuyuki finds a shirt she wants. Something in Japanese and a couple of kid characters from a cartoon I've never watched.

"I'm going to buy it big so you can wear it too," she says.

I laugh as she moves by. I'm never wearing that.

She gets into a long conversation with the shop owner. She talks about a series he's never seen and never will from another dimension. He's clueless and enthralled. After ringing up the shirt, he gives her a deep discount. She pays but seems to get more money back than what she gave him. They talk for a while and I keep looking around. This place is a shrine to heroes I'll never know.

"Joe." I look up and she's near the door waving at me to hurry.

I nod and leave. The owner gives me a high-five. Weird, friendly people in this world.

"You could become a writer in California and make these shows," the owner says as we walk out.

She's thinking about that. The stadium gates open. "We better get in," Nobuyuki says.

"Did he give you too much money back?" I ask as we move.

"No," Nobuyuki says flatly.

I hoped that the shop owner paid her for the ideas that he writes to the next level of fandom. We're already at the gate and she hands the tickets to an old lady with a weird electronic box. She scans the tickets and we're in.

"Enjoy the game," she says as we move in.

There is a wall of team merchandise as we enter. Hometown pride for a little baseball team that could. Their winning seasons are posted all over the park. We get into the concessions line and she orders nachos, hot dogs, and drinks. Brands are different, but logos are similar. We take the food and find our seats left of home plate and in the first ten rows. We sit. Immediately, two older men lean forward to tell me these are Marvin's seats.

"He gave us the tickets. I got a haircut today. He's got a hot date."

The old man roars with laughter. "Hey, everyone." He announces, "They're Marvin's customers, and he's got a hot date." The entire section applauds. We're strangers sitting in a group of regulars.

Tonight, the hometown Bottle Caps are playing the South Bend Grizzlies. A man with a radio voice announces the players as they run on the field. They line up and a small gal approaches. The inhabitants of the stadium stand. She sings the national anthem. It sounds right. She hits all the notes, but the lines seem different.

"They got a good one tonight," the old man says behind me. I nod.

We sit and they go through a load of announcements and team schedules as the teams warm up. It's a nice evening with just a hint of cold wind. I'm staring off into space when the action begins. There are old memories here. I excuse myself and get up. Nobuyuki questions me, but I pat her on the head and go. I walk to the top of the stairs, turn, and look. The tsunami of memories is on the horizon. A section over third base calls to me. There are empty seats. I walk over, sit, and the tsunami washes over me.

I've been here before. My leg crosses and my left arm goes out over the seatback. I used to be here with someone. I look over and into the void.

There is the crack of the bat. Luckily, a fast kid with a mitt sits in front of me. He catches the ball that probably would have smacked me in the head. I give him a high five and move back to the regular seats. I sit next to Nobuyuki.

"These seats are not good enough for you?" the old man behind me asks.

"These are great seats. Had an old ghost I needed to talk to."

"Dad?" Nobuyuki is wondering if we should go. "Is everything okay?"

"Yeah. Had some old memories, like really old memories pop up. I think I've been here before."

"You from Fort Wayne?" the old man asks behind me.

"Just passing through."

"I like it here," Nobuyuki says.

"Here if you want to put down some roots." The old man passes us a business card. "I own rental houses if you look to settle down. You seem like good people."

Nobuyuki takes an immediate interest in the old man, but I stop her. My sense of trust is waning. She's staring at me with sad eyes. "One month," she says. "We need to settle for a while and let our bodies rest."

"We don't know this place well enough," I cut her off. The old man touches my shoulder.

"I've been here all my life except for six years that I

flew in Cambodia during the war. It's a good city. Schools are strong and they have lots to do here. You'd be hard-pressed to find a better town to raise a kid."

That makes me laugh. "She raises me more than I raise her."

The old man turns to Nobuyuki. "You'd be hard-pressed to find a better place to raise a grown man."

Nobuyuki touches my hand. I ignore the old man and watch the game. Nobuyuki and the old man talk about the town, where his houses are, and she schedules a viewing tomorrow.

I sigh.

"Your secretary made an appointment. If you need work, several folks in this section own businesses. They're always on the lookout for someone new. The town's growing and doing well."

Nobuyuki banters with the old man and elbows me in the side.

"Al's got a rental that's fully furnished. He's going to let us stay there a couple of days and we can check out the town. We can stay if we're happy with it," she's whispering the information to me. Al, she's already on a first-name basis. He's doomed. "And it's near a school!" she exclaims loudly. Like she could sit in a room with children and learn basic math.

The old man clasps my shoulder. "This kid is one of the best barterers I've talked to." Totally doomed.

"She's got an old soul," I respond. "And a strong poker face, be careful."

They continue talking and I watch the game. The Bottle Caps are doing okay until the bottom of the fourth. Bases loaded, and a home run ruins the outlook.

"Bah," the old man yells. "This game's over."

Nobuyuki must be on the same frequency. "Is this why Marvin gave us the tickets?"

The old man laughs. "Yeah, he knew this was a no-win situation. If you want, I can take you over to the house, so you can see it in the light."

I've had my baseball fix for the day. "Yeah, I'm good."

We get up to go. On the way out, he introduces me to a man named Marty.

"Old Al is picking up strangers again, eh," Marty says. Marty looks busy and eternally tired. I can't tell if he's got more hair on his head or on his ears.

Al fills them in on our "story". Nobuyuki was busy and I nod while taking mental notes. I have strong accounting skills and know all the programs.

"I own a place at One Summit Square. Come see me and let's talk about a job. How about tomorrow at 1 PM." He hands me a business card.

I hesitate and Nobuyuki slightly kicks me again. I take the business card and shake his hand. "Yes, I'll be there. Thank you, sir."

Al pats me on the shoulder. "Did you guys walk or drive?"

"We walked," I answer.

"I got room in the truck." We walk out of the park and go to a quad cab. He drives through a town he's lived in all his life and is proud of. Al points out a grocery store and the schools nearby. Down a couple of side streets, we find a nice bungalow with a cool porch. The lights are on and it looks homey.

He pulls into the driveway and shuts off the truck. "This used to be my sister's home. She was never one for kids and left everything to me when she died a couple of years ago. I had my place and put this one up for rent. A single lady rented here for a while, met some fella online, and moved out of the country. She left everything and was a clean freak. So there isn't anything you need."

I can't tell if he's talking to me or Nobuyuki.

"Here are the rules: no parties, no drugs, no loud music, no big dogs unless you clear it with me first. If you make a mess, clean it up. If you break it, replace it. I also recommend tenant's insurance." He opened the door and it felt like home. It didn't feel elderly. It felt like a place to eat supper and relax. If it had ghosts, Nobuyuki would take care of them quickly.

"Oh, there is no cable."

"What about internet?" I ask.

Al tilts his head toward me. "Everywhere has internet. You just plug in the BlackBox. You'll have to get one. I thought everyone had one." Al shrugs. "The previous owner took hers."

"Oh, I'll pick it up." Nobuyuki laughs. "He doesn't know electronics. I'll take care of it."

Al pats her head. "You're a good kid to have around." She gives a hug and snags Al, hook, line, and sinker.

"The house has three bedrooms, two bathrooms, and a fairly generous backyard. Just take good care and clean up any messes," Al says. "I have the utilities under my name. If you decide to stay more than a week, then we can talk about a longer lease."

Nobuyuki approaches him. She hands him money. "This will hold us for the week," she says, touching Al's shoulder.

"Yep, this will hold you for the week, little lady."

They shake hands. "Joe, my number is on the

business card. Contact me if you need anything."

"Thank you for everything, Al."

"Sure thing, sir. Don't forget Marty tomorrow at 1 PM."

"I won't."

"All right, kids. Have a good night. I'll stop by tomorrow at 5 PM and see if you need anything."

Al waves at us and walks out. We stand at the window and watch the truck pull out of the driveway.

"How much did you give him for the week?"

"Enough, we still need groceries."

"He's a good guy. Don't use him."

"I didn't." It's flat and I've poked the bear that's been hanging around all day. "I'll make it up to him. Why are you so untrusting of me? Three years of survival and now you're suddenly questioning my motives?" She's staring at me and her eyes are narrow, locked, and getting darker. Her skin shimmers and grows. Suddenly, old man Nobuyuki stands before me.

"I don't enjoy people standing over me," Nobuyuki says.

I step back.

"What did you read in the library, Joe?"

"A book on folklore."

"Ah, that explains why you've been acting so weird. Understand this, Joe. Folklore is lies from ancient times. Usually from the victors of war. My clan didn't fare well in conflicts. We had low standing, and they called us thieves and monsters."

"You stole from people today."

"I didn't steal. I bartered. Would you rather go live on the streets?" The old man's eyes are totally black and it's unnerving. He motions at the door. "The door is right there. If we stay, we could be here for a long time. Al will get paid back many times over."

I stare out the window for a while. The old man glares at me in the reflection.

"We're multiverse nomads, you and I. We've possibly found a place where everything isn't trying to kill us. Let's take a breather and live for a while. This world is fairly normal. Please, let's just try it out."

"Okay." I walk away and go into the backyard.

The sun's gone down and the first stars are out. There's a comfortable table and chair I ease into. I look up. The stars look different here, but there is no frame of reference. A sense of normal would be nice. There's a slight breeze and the temperature is just right.

I'm tired, but need to come up with some things, like a resume and credible back story. Lies will get us caught, but the truth is too strange. If I lie, what am I doing yelling at Nobuyuki trying to get us to survive a strange world?

Being an interdimensional hobo is hard work and not for the faint of heart.

There's movement by the door and I glance to see Nobuyuki standing there. She's back in her little girl form. I pull up the other deck chair. She comes out and sits cautiously.

"I'm sorry, Nobuyuki."

She nods, sits in the chair, and kicks her legs.

"We need groceries."

"I need to come up with a story for a resume. Do you remember how to get to the store from here?"

"Yes. Let's go."

Al left the keys on the table. I'm not used to keys and am afraid I may lose them. We lock up and leave the house. 1718, I look at the house number. We pass a street sign. Fairview. I have an address. "1718 Fairview, I have an address. I am somebody," I say.

Nobuyuki giggles and takes my hand. She adjusts her grip a few times. It's cautious. We walk in silence to the store. I try not to think too deeply.

There is a typical supermarket not too far away. Light beige walls, white floors, incandescent lighting that makes everything too bright. I grab a cart. Nobuyuki is calculating the moment we walk in the store. She pulls on the front of the cart like a tugboat and leads the expedition. She grabs some outdated berries, a big thing of cereal, milk, bread, eggs, sausage, and hamburger. I'm not paying very much attention until Nobuyuki has a catch in her breath.

"What's wrong?"

She sniffles, locks her body, and is about ready to go into epic breakdown mode.

"This used to be our thing," she says in halting breaths. "Before you lost your memories." I don't remember if Nobuyuki ever cried in front of me. "We loved going to the grocery store together."

"It's okay." I hold her close in a hug. Patting this little trembling mess.

"I wish you would remember, Joe. The brands are so close. This is so close to home."

Her heart's hammering. "What's wrong?"

"I don't want to fight. I don't like fighting, I like surviving. I'm so tired of running."

"No extermination squads or dragons?"

"No."

I let her cry for a bit, then wipe the tears from her eyes.

117

"I want to go back to simple," she says.

"You're boring, Nobuyuki."

"And that's okay." She squeezes me in a bear hug. I'm glad she's the little girl. If she was the old man, this would have been awkward. "We can survive boring," she says.

"Come on, let's finish up."

We hit a few more things.

"There was a coffee maker back at the house?"

"Yes."

"Most excellent." I go for a sniff test down the coffee aisle. There's a simple bag claiming to be a local coffee roaster. It smells like morning. I put it in the basket and we go to check out. Nobuyuki takes charge. She spins the cart away from the lane that I was going to.

"Problem?" I ask.

"No, let's check out over here." Nobuyuki forces the cart in her direction.

"No line over this way." I stop the cart.

"I'm free over on register four," a familiar voice calls out.

I look up and recognize the long-haired brunette. "Over here, Nobuyuki."

She hesitates and lets go. "I'm going to check out the BlackBox. Here is enough money as long as taxes don't kill us."

"You must be new here. We don't charge taxes on regular groceries," the clerk says.

Nobuyuki walks away to the courtesy booth and talks with the person behind the counter.

The brunette rings up the groceries. "Haven't seen you in here before. Where y'all from?"

"A little all over. We just got into Fort Wayne

today."

"Welcome to Fort Wayne. Usually not a destination place, but it will do."

"Sounds like a good slogan. Come to Fort Wayne, it will do."

I look at her name tag. Nat. Not Natalie or some other name, just simple Nat. The name tag looks a little worn. She's been here for a while. She is a familiar. When she glances up at me, I see Rebecca and it crushes me.

"Have you been to Fort Wayne before?"

"Off and on in my life," I lie.

"Now that you've stood here a moment, you look familiar." She has a slight southern drawl she hides well.

"I get that a lot, but you do too."

"Where did you go to school?"

"Not here."

She smiles and gives me the total. Nobuyuki nailed it.

The groceries are bagged and ready.

"Thanks, Nat."

"Sure thing, come back, and I'll ask you lots more questions about your life you don't want to answer." Her smile promises a lot of mischief.

I smile back. Part of me wants to blurt out something dumb when Nobuyuki kicks my foot.

"Ready?"

She's got a sack of her own and she pulls me out of the store. She's waiting to say something.

"Rebecca."

"She's slightly different this time. Just remember, she's not always a positive in the world."

"Stay away?" I stress the last of it too much and

sound like a whiney middle schooler.

"Yes, please stay away."

"Do I have to?" My question trails off into the night as we pass the large parking lot, cross the street, and wander into the neighborhoods.

A dog barks nearby and Nobuyuki bumps into me.

"You okay?"

"I hate dogs."

I look down. Her fox tails are hanging out.

"Um, Nobuyuki." I point.

"Sorry, that happens when I get startled." The tails draw up and disappear.

She moves to the other side of the street away from the fence, holding back the barking dog.

"So, no pets?"

She doesn't answer and bolts away.

I can't keep up, but we're at the house in no time. There is a box on the front porch. A note on top of it says to look through it and see if there is anything we need from Al. The guy couldn't be nicer. I take it in and unpack. Canned goods and other things to make our lives easier.

I put the groceries away. She already has the BlackBox plugged in and programming a smart phone. She looks at the screen and passes it to me.

"We need to build you a resume. Look up recently bankrupt businesses. Push the search date back a couple of years." I'm a monkey trying to work a remote control but I find a very familiar name.

"Did I ever talk about a business called Midwest Visions?"

Nobuyuki is furiously working on another phone. "I don't think so. Where was it at?"

"Michigan Power Center."

Nobuyuki stops and looks at me. "You've got a strange attraction to that place. Maybe that's why. Look it up."

There is an old dead website. This was a business that worked with local officials to bring in innovative companies. I look through the contacts and nothing pops out at me. The CEO's picture stops me cold. The elderly form of Nobuyuki stares at me through the screen.

"What is it?" Nobuyuki asks. "You've gone pale."

I hold the phone out for her to see.

"Whoa," she says. "I've never been here before."

"Could it be another of your kind?"

"Doubtful. Our forms are distinct. If it was another, I'd feel them close by."

"How do you get your form?"

"They come with age. There are different tales about it."

"Like?" I ask too fast. My tone is too defensive and I try to smooth it out.

"It's different for my kind. It can be someone we met in an encounter, someone we loved and followed, sometimes it may be someone that did us wrong."

"How did you become the old man?"

"It just happened. I never met him, then one day found I could shift to that body."

"And the form you're in now?"

"This was my original form. It happened earlier than it should."

I stare at her, not sure what to say. "You can't manifest the old man while we are here."

I copy the old man's name and do a quick search. There was a terrible wreck, but the police could not locate the body. I stare at the picture. Something is familiar.

Nobuyuki moves to me. I want to flinch away but stop myself.

I show her the phone. She takes it, scans the article, and her fingers fly on my phone.

"If there is a problem, I can only manifest the sword as the old man. I can fight in this form, but not with the lethal advantage." She has the look from the grocery store right before she broke down. "Should we leave?"

"Do you think we're in danger?" I ask not knowing whether to trust her new emotions.

"I think we're in a safe place," she says. There's a hint of inflection on the end. "Their news is full of warm stories. Fluffy pieces, but might be a slow news day."

She hands the phone back to me. "I'm comfortable in this form and have survived in it for a long time. The only problem is, it doesn't age."

"Could be a problem, long term. But we've done it before, right?"

Nobuyuki nods.

"Let's get settled before we worry too much."

She goes back to punching things into her phone. "Good catch on the old man."

"I think I'm going to go to sleep." The phone is already giving me a headache. "I'll get up early and hit the library."

"Okay, good night." She's in a corner chair, face lit up by the pale artificial light. Her fingers fly.

I go into the master bedroom. The linens are clean, but I'm sleeping in someone's bed and it's a little weird. I'm listening to the house, every little pop and groan as it settles into the nighttime air and the central heat comes on. *What am I going to do for a work history? Do I even give him a resume that can be tracked down as lies?* I stare at the ceiling as I try to set an alarm on the phone. The lights in the house go out and the door across the hall opens. A moment later, my door slides open. Nobuyuki is in her dark fox form.

"Do you mind if I sleep in here? The room is too weird and I'm still used to the void."

"Sure."

They jump up on the chair in the room. Tries to circle and finds it useless. Nobuyuki sighs and jumps up to the foot of the bed.

"What am I going to do for a resume?" I ask.

"We will make something up. Don't worry about it too much. I made up a brief work history."

"You got this?"

"Yes, and only a few things to remember."

The bed seems to give a little and I relax a little more. I'm comforted by the heater's hum and fall to sleep. My dreams hit quickly. Someone's next to me, a gossamer form of Nat from the grocery store. She glows red and touches me. The light spreads through me and is warm.

Memories hit me. Nat's in a car with me, but it's not her. There's a squeal of tires and I yell.

She comforts me, holds me, and tells me it's okay. "It's just a nightmare," she whispers.

I'm diving into a bottomless ocean and remember dragons, blood, and the Yurei from the cold worlds. Sancho Tom talks to me as the moon destroys the Earth. Scenes quickly change.

There is another dream. The Michigan Power Building stands in the distance. Something hits the back of my head, and I fall. I fall into the void. I'm seated in an office. The office girl walks by with a stack of folders, but she doesn't scream. It's a good place. I'm working on the MacMurray account. The taxes are crazy and they're trying to hide something that will get them in trouble with the IRS. I found the issue and they're doing everything to cover it up. There's a big cup of coffee on my desk with some odd cartoon characters. I look at their bank accounts and trace money going to an offshore account. I have them red-handed.

Nat whispers, "Remember."

I miss her, then forget her.

I sit up in sweat-soaked sheets. Nobuyuki is in her fox form in the corner, a flowing mass of darkness in an already dark room.

"Joe?"

Her eyes open. The fiery pits stare through me.

"Nightmare," I grunt. I get up and go to the kitchen for a glass of water. I bump into everything as I maneuver through a dark house I don't know. Nobuyuki hits a light and is back in the little girl form.

"Ouch, a little warning next time."

"Get your water. It's 3 AM. Nothing's up but ghosts," she says and turns off the lights.

There is someone I forget. *Who was the girl in the grocery store?* I lie down. The bed's sweaty but large enough that I move to the cold side. I stare at the ceiling in the dark until the darkness calls me again for another dream.

I'm sitting in an office working with the door open, listening to the office traffic. People walk by and nod, ghostly faces, but not much more. The computer in front of me shows several spreadsheets and I understand the flow. Accounting suddenly seems second nature. I try to focus on an award with a business name and hear the squealing of tires behind my desk. The world is spinning around us and look at a woman's horrified face. The world spins and I'm upside down. I barely open one eye and can't feel anything else. Something carries me away. I try to reach out, but my arm doesn't respond. "Rebecca," I mumble as the red glow comes back. I yell and fall back into nothing.

I'm dreaming within my dream. Old man Nobuyuki mutters things to me as I remember past events. I sit at my desk with my coffee cup, surrounded by the abyss. Everything is dark, but I still hear Nobuyuki whispering. The words don't make sense and before long, I'm floating alone in the void.

My alarm makes me jump and it's barely light outside. Nobuyuki's not in the room. I roll on my back and rub my eyes. It's been a while since I've heard an alarm and try to remember how to stop it. I get up and go through the morning routine. In the kitchen, old man Nobuyuki cooks breakfast.

He looks at me. "I know, but we're in the house and no one can see me. It's too hard reaching the shelves in the other form."

He has eggs and sausage almost ready and it smells wonderful. There is a cup of coffee waiting.

"This is awesome, Nobuyuki. Thank you."

"We need to get you ready for your big day."

We eat and go through a pot of coffee quickly. Dishes are quick. Nobuyuki forms into the little girl.

"I got to find some clothes," I say.

We finish what we need to do and head out into the city. It's a slow walk downtown from the house. We pass a second-hand clothing store and go in. There are several different sets of outfits and dress clothes in my size. I decide on some not too out of date. Since my sense of fashion is from another universe, I ask the lady running the register if this looked good for an interview.

"I'd hire you." It's something said several times before. "You want to wear it outside?"

I nod and she takes all the tags off and rolls a lint remover over the dress jacket.

Nobuyuki pays her and she wishes me luck. I hit the dressing room and change into the new wardrobe.

We head into the library and before long, Nobuyuki and I have drafted a resume.

"Can I do this?" I ask Nobuyuki.

Nothing like making up a last name. I'm not sure if I could find the house.

She smiles. "This is a formality. Marty will hire you on the spot and you'll be working today. If you do, please don't worry about me."

This doesn't feel right, but I try not to look worried.

"It's a new town and I'll keep myself busy. I will find you this afternoon when you get off."

We hit print and ask for an envelope from the desk clerk. There is about an hour to kill before I need to go and we wander the library for a little while. Nobuyuki finds a large book of history and falls in. I find a book of history too. I read about thirty minutes while nervously looking at a clock. There's a map book on a nearby table and I look for places of residency. Kansas is right in the middle of the country and Topeka is on a highway. Sounds good. I touch Nobuyuki's shoulder. "I'll call you."

She looks up, nods, and goes back to the book.

I take my resume and walk down the block.

As I get close to the Michigan Power Center, someone yells my name. I'm looking around trying to find Al, about the only person I know in this world. There is a young Mexican man in his twenties calling out to me. He looks familiar, but I can't place him. I walk over.

"How are you, Joe? Haven't seen you in a while."

I'm eyeing him suspiciously. He reaches out and shakes my hand. He drops the happy façade immediately once he touches my hand. I remember his name.

"Sancho Tom."

"She's bad for you. She's erasing you bit by bit."

I let his hand go. "I have to go."

"Look at you, all gussied up. Do you have an interview?" He smiles.

"Yeah."

He hands me a card. "Just in case you need a reference to back up a credible back story."

"Thanks." I retreat, needing to make my appointment.

"Good luck, buddy. Stop by later, by yourself."

Sancho Tom, even the card looks familiar. I've got a little time before the interview as I enter the lobby. Once in, I'm hit with more déjà vu. The outside of this place remains the same in most worlds, but I rarely go inside. I always thought there was too much wood in the foyer. The backboards to the security station almost look like a judge's bench and it makes me shudder. I look at the card Marty gave me. The company is his full name "and associates, LLC" at the end.

At the elevators, I find Marty on the list among banking locations, utility companies, doctor offices, and other names. My hands are sweaty as I hit the elevator button. I'm not ready to settle down yet. This isn't home. This could be a trap. My mind rattles.

I walk back into the lobby. The large board behind the security station has the skyscraper logo, but it's different. It's no longer the Michigan Power Building but One Summit Square.

"Can I help you?" The guard looks up from the desk and his paper.

"Sorry, just looking around."

"Are you here to see someone?"

"I've got an appointment with Marty Gordon and Associates…LLC. I'm just killing time."

The guard stands up and walks over. "Ah, Marty is a good guy. You interviewing?"

"Yes."

"I can tell you're a little nervous. Marty is a great guy." He puts his hand out.

We shake hands.

"I'm Mike," the guard says.

This Mike is in his forties, a big strong guy, somewhat familiar but not quite. He's not a Mike I've seen before.

"Hey there, I'm Joe." Mike looks at me oddly.

"Have I seen you around?"

"It's weird. My first time here, but I know where everything is."

"That's a good sign. It means you're welcome here. I need to walk around. Want to go see Marty?"

I look at the clock. I either do the interview or go out in the street and jump in the trash cart. "Yeah, let's do this."

"There you go, buddy. You got this." Mike pats me

on the shoulder as we walk over to the elevators and he hits the button.

The door dings and the office girl comes out. My usual barometer. She doesn't have files.

She smiles at Mike and me.

"Hey, Sarah. Tom's set up down the street."

"I saw that. Do you want anything?" she calls back.

"Nah, I'll go down in a little bit."

We enter the elevator.

"Sancho Tom?" I ask.

The guard laughs. "Oh yeah. Good food and a nice kid running it. He's going places with that food truck."

I nod as the elevator rises.

"Not scared of heights, are you?"

"Not particularly?" I lie and Mike knows. Right now, I'm scared of everything.

"I wouldn't look down when we get up here. Above the 34th floor, people get a little panicky."

"Great."

We go straight up. A bell rings and the door opens.

"Now that's service," Mike says and walks out. "Come here." He walks down a hall to an open courtyard. There are marks on the floor that may have held a small coffee shop or grab-and-go food place. He looks at the floor and sticks his arms out like he's balancing on a tightrope. "Yep, right here."

He steps off and I walk over.

"Put your hands out like I had them and tip your head back a little."

I do and immediately don't like the sensation. I'm swaying.

"Please don't tell me that's the building moving," I ask.

129

"Oh yeah. That's the building moving."

"What are you doing to my young upstart, Mike?" Marty stands out in the hall. He looks like a little goblin statue. He's leaning on a cane as he approaches us and pats Mike on the back.

"Hello, Joe. Is Mike leaving you alone?"

"He's introducing me to the building's sway."

"Oh, you get used to it. As long as you're not afraid of heights." He pauses and looks up at me, laughing. "Don't worry, you'll get over it. Just don't stand near the windows the first couple of weeks."

"I got to get back to the station. You guys have a good day," Mike says.

I shake his hand and thank him for delivering me. He looks at the old man, then back to me smiling. "Good luck."

"Come on in," Marty says and I slowly follow into the office. Marty Gordan and Associates LLC is announced in gold and black stencil on the window. The place smells like paper and unsmoked cigars. It's a little warm with the sun shining through and feels homey. There is a large meeting room up front that passes into another office. Marty limps over to the desk and hops up a little in his chair. The light coming in from the window catches the fuzz around his ears and gives him an almost radiant look.

He looks at me for a moment.

"Al likes you and your daughter a lot. I've never seen him take care of people like that, including his grandkids."

I nod. "The house was unexpected."

"Your little girl told him quite the story. You guys have been moving around a lot since the accident."

I catch my breath.

"Al told me. There was a bad car wreck, traumatic injuries, and missing time. You've been drifting."

I apologize, but Marty holds his hand out for me to stop.

"That doesn't matter. Al says you are a gifted accountant and I can use one. I want to see something. There is a set of books in the office next door and a computer if you need to look up anything specifically. I want to see if anything strikes you as odd with the bookkeeping."

"It's been a while," I sigh.

"I know. Just take a look and see. If you need to take a break, bathrooms are down the hall. If you get hungry or thirsty, let me know. You are my guest and I will take care of you. Take all the time you need."

"Got any coffee?"

"Of course, we got coffee." There's a tone in his voice like I just asked for air. "Want anything in it?"

"Nope."

"Get to work. I'll bring you a cup."

I walk over to the next office. There are ledgers on the shelf and desk. The computer is on and logged in with the accounting system. The books are written in an old man's handwriting and the shaky penmanship is hard to read. Then the letters and numbers shift to a young girl's handwriting. Within a couple of pages, I'm already finding inaccuracies between the ledgers and the computer. I'm writing them out when Marty walks in with a steaming cup of coffee.

"This is a place we represent and sell." Marty stops and glances at my notes. "They roast their own coffee. The guy has some incredible beans he imports."

I stop for a moment and take a drink. It's hot, but the richness of the coffee flows over me.

"Wow."

"Yeah, that's why I picked them up as a client. We're going to distribute them across the state in a couple of weeks. I think in a year, we will take them nationally."

I push the paper at him. "What's Jamellacor?"

Marty laughs. "It's a false company that one of my associates was funneling about a half cent on every dollar I spent."

I know this accounting system on the computer and scrub for metadata. The computer's thinking. It brings up all Jamellacor interactions for the last year.

Marty limps around. "Can you expand that to a five-year window?"

I enter more code. Results from the last three years pop up.

Marty sighs and curses under his breath. "There was a kid I hired a while back, out of school. She was a strong accountant. Great gal, fun to have in the office. I planned on leaving all this to her one day. She was my right hand around here. I loved her like a daughter and she used me."

He pauses and I look up. Tears well in his eyes. "Please print that." Marty clears his throat. "We need to go see someone."

I print off the documents and notice something. There's another holding company sneaking through the pages.

"Give me a moment, Marty."

I enter another odd code into the search and pull up some more interactions. Less in interactions, higher in money.

Marty's looking through his trifocals and he trembles through the desk.

"This is all new, Joe. You are gifted at this."

The path didn't go too much further. There were dummy corporations made up and funneled through. Somewhat hidden and not carelessly left in the open. Finally, I'm able to dive deeper and see the checks cut to the company. I'm putting names into the Federal Trade Commission's website and it's coming up blank. Marty wanders off and brings me a fresh mug of coffee. He's superpowering my work. We sit there for hours. I pull together the information and print it out. Marty shuffles in and out.

"Anything else?" Marty seems older than when I came in.

"I can look again, but pretty sure this is everything."

I lay it out on the desk and trace where the side money went. Marty doesn't want to look at it.

"I made a call. Do you mind seeing someone with me?" Marty paces and this isn't how I viewed my first day. There's a thundercloud over the building.

"Did I do something wrong?" I ask.

Marty's anger cracks. "No, son. You've done everything to a degree that I should be ashamed of. I paid others good money to dig through this and not find anything beyond what we already knew. I'm only mad at myself."

"It was well hidden, don't be."

Marty paces, trying to figure out what to do next. He wants to cuss and yell.

"Should we go?"

"Yes, we should." He walks to the front as I gather

all the papers. By the time I make the front door, he's putting on a jacket and hat. We take the elevator down a couple of floors. It's a legal office.

A voice yells out from an office. "You know I wanted to go home at some point, Marty."

I recognize the man from the baseball game.

"Ah, your new progeny. Hey, Joe. Did Al treat you right?" He gets up and shakes Marty's hand, then mine.

"Al did me a big favor, Gary. I want to show you what Joe found."

We go into his office. Books are everywhere, mostly large tomes of legal cases and law.

We sit at a conference table and I show the path Jamellacor took the last couple of years. Gary calculates and nods. He's seen this before. Then I show him some of the dummy corporations.

"Investigative accounting brought down the mob. Good job, Joe." Gary says, going over the papers.

I sit back when my presentation is over and let Marty and Gary talk. They discuss wire fraud and several new possibilities.

Gary sat back and looked grim. "This could mean a lot of time."

Marty looked at the desk, nodding. Tears were filling his eyes.

Gary gets up and walks to the door of the office. "Joe, if you don't mind. Can Marty and I have an off-the-books discussion?"

"Sure." I go back to the entrance and find a chair. I hear voices, sometimes angry, sometimes understanding, one time pleading. This is killing Marty.

The door opens and Gary walks out. Marty struggles behind him.

"I would have given this all to her, but instead she took bits and pieces behind my back. It hurt me."

Gary pats Marty on the back. "I'll get the paperwork started. Might need some signatures later this week." They walk to the front of Gary's office and he pushes a box of tissues to Marty. He takes one and makes a sound like an angry goose.

Gary walks around the table and shakes my hand. "I may need to borrow you from time to time. People love stealing money in very sneaky ways."

"He's my resource. You ask nicely," Marty says.

"I'll pay him and give you bourbon, old man." Gary laughs.

Marty looks at his watch. "It's getting late and I'm keeping you from your little girl. Great work for your first day. You're hired."

I shake Marty's hand. "Thanks. When do you want me here tomorrow?"

Marty looks serious. "Take a couple of days and the weekend to get settled." He pulls out a wallet and hands me a stack of bills. "Come back Tuesday and we'll talk business. This legal mumbo-jumbo is going to take some time to unravel and there is no point in you sitting in an office without something to do."

I try to hand the money back.

"That's yours, Joe. I'll pay you for the week. Come back, and we'll discuss salary. You helped me more than you know and I owe Al for sending you to me." Marty takes my hands with both of his. "I'm going to sit here for a bit and contemplate my business failings. See you soon."

I leave and Gary walks me out into the hallway. "Take good care of him, Joe. Marty has a big, dumb heart. Don't take advantage."

I nod. "I just need something to get on my feet."

Gary smiles. "Oh, buddy. You're hip-deep just to get back on your feet. Marty is looking for someone to mentor. Be good to him. You'll learn a lot and earn the keys to the kingdom."

Gary eyes me as I say goodbye from the hallway. The elevator is not too far away and I head to the ground floor. I've ridden in this elevator thousands of times and look for familiar scratches on the brass plates, knowing they're there, but can't find them. This is a replica home in a new development. It's too clean. The elevator stops a few times and people get on and off. Typical busy place. I've had too much coffee and no lunch. The sun is behind the building and already looks dark outside. I reach for my phone to call Nobuyuki but look down the street. Sancho Tom's Taco Truck is still there. My thoughts wander as I walk down.

There is a big sign on the menu that says, "Sancho Tom's is Sold Out. I'll be back tomorrow with more." Tom works in the truck, moving stuff around, and glances out at me. He holds a finger up, asking me to wait. It's been a good first day. I look around, thinking how lucky we've been here. A random meeting with a barber led to a baseball game, a house, and a full-time job.

Tom exits and smiles at me. He walks over and gives me a handshake.

"You have no idea who I am, do you?" asks Tom.

"Taco truck guy who gave me a card earlier. You look familiar." I let go of his hand.

"My friend, you are in some serious danger. It's taking parts of you."

"What are you talking about?"

"Try something for me, buddy. Think about the plague planet."

I step back.

"I know who you are and your powers, Joe. What concerns me is you're missing time and the company you keep loves to eat memories. Can you remember?"

"Yes."

He points over to the park nearby. "That was full of memorial plague pits."

I nod.

"You see the turnabout there?" He motions over to the large street with a circle embedded in it.

"Yes."

"Remember." It's a simple request. I'm walking with Nobuyuki and we look up. I'm trying to run the memory, but the next thing I remember is walking to the Michigan Power Center to leave.

"Think about that again." He puts a hand in the center of my back.

I'm walking to the Plague Pit Memorial. Tom's hand sends mild shocks racing through me. I'm looking at the area he pointed out. There is a big void of darkness around it that shatters. It reforms and Nobuyuki and I walk away. There is a Styrofoam box on the ground. Tom takes his hand off my back. He moves into his truck and pulls out a Styrofoam box. "Here. I gave you a free meal. I did that day too."

"Oh, thanks." I devour the tacos.

Tom watches me eat. "You're missing the point. You are missing time because it feeds on memories, my friend."

"How do you know this?" I ask licking the salsa and

grease from my fingers.

"I'm a traveler too." Tom says. "And I've seen similar things before."

"You're like me?"

Tom laughs. "No, not like you. I'm kind of everywhere."

"Can you get me home?"

He touches my back again and I'm filled with visions. I'm staring at the faceless one that tried to make it in the cart with me.

"Oh, you nearly had contact. You really don't know what you're doing."

My memories move around. I'm in the void, staring at Nobuyuki in her dark form.

"I knew it," Tom says, "She's a Nogitsune. That's the worst type."

I move and the contact breaks. "I've got to go."

"You're in danger, pal. If you stay with her, it's going to keep feeding on you. It may help you now, but those things are parasites. Keep it around and you will die."

"Can you get me home?"

Tom shrugs. "I'll have to study you longer. I looked at your memories, but didn't get far enough. That may take some time."

"I'll find you, and we will talk."

"Get rid of it tonight, Joe. You're in danger."

I walk away. Near the park, I turn toward the library. Nobuyuki sits on the stairs reading.

"How did it go?" she asks.

"It was a highly successful day. I solved a problem he's been dealing with and he gave me until Tuesday to settle in. Then we talk about salary."

Nobuyuki squeals. She pops up, grabs my hand, and we're walking. I think about what Sancho Tom said. She's babbling in excited child speak and I'm not listening. She's been going through history books and this seems to be a very normal world. News is boring, the economy is good, everyone seems healthy.

She tells me about another park she went to and met other kids. She's falling into the role. A sweet, ancient, possibly malign spirit is playing with children. There was a pause. She tugs on my hand. "We need to get some clothes."

"I got paid, but let's not go too crazy."

"We got money." She's been hunting while I was working. "There are some clothing stores ahead downtown," she says.

We walk around and find the pop-culture store.

"I want to go back in." She drops my hand and doesn't wait for permission.

I wander around the storefronts and go in a little later. She's in deep conversation over this imaginary show the owner has never seen. There's a play-by-play of each character. I walk to the back and there's a group playing some role-playing game. They look at me like a door knock during a séance.

One of them uncomfortably says hello.

"Hey," I answer back. Now their game is fully on pause.

There are computers linked up to play and I take a seat. Before long, I'm blasting aliens or demons or hybrids of both. They go back to their game and keep a wary eye my way. I'm dying quick. One of the kids points out the controller layout. He takes my controller and pulls up a menu. He's rattling off things I don't understand trying to walk me through it.

"Okay."

I go back and do better, but there is a pile of my bodies beneath me and it becomes the hill I'm dying on. He takes my controller, resets the game on easy, and starts it over. The tutorial takes over and I lose a little time. I'm hungry again but can't go to Tom's with Nobuyuki. I get up and mumble thanks to the kids.

Nobuyuki is deep in plot development and the owner is furiously scribbling notes.

"Let's go get dinner," I say to Nobuyuki.

"There's a great burger place about a block down." The owner points.

"You staying?"

Nobuyuki nods.

"I'll be back."

The streets are quiet for a Monday evening. No baseball game, so nobody's wandering around. I find the burger place and it's mostly empty. It's basic, but they also have a fancier menu where they call mayo, aioli. I go with a regular cheeseburger. My eyes drift to the fancy menu with a breakfast burger featuring an egg, bacon, and hash browns. It has garlic aioli which adds several bucks to it.

I pull out the money and look at it. It has some presidents I recall, typical landmarks, odd anti-counterfeiting measures. I don't remember what a bill originally looked like, so I don't know what I'm looking for.

The waitress brings me a drink. "Just print those?" she asks as I look at the twenty dollars.

I laugh. "No, they're good."

She doesn't share the mirth, stares at me for a

moment, and walks away. I put the money in my pocket and my hand bumps into Sancho Tom's card.

I pull it out and look at it. *You're in danger.* The words rattle around. I zoned out because the waitress stands there with the burger and fries.

"Everything okay, sir?" she asks as she sets the plate in front of me.

"Everything is great. Thanks for asking. It's been a long day."

"Need anything else?"

"No, I'm good."

I put the card away and eat. It's a good burger, not out of this world, but will do for supper. Someone walks in. Nobuyuki slips in the chair next to me. She's got a bag with her. Shopping? "Yes, and that was supposed to be the focus tonight. If you hurry up, there's another place we can hit before they close."

She helps herself to my fries. "You want anything?"

"No, I'm good. The owner wants to help me write the series I've been telling him about. I'm kind of excited."

"This world has been good for you."

"And you too. So far, nothing is chasing us."

I inhale the burger, while Nobuyuki finishes most of the fries. The waitress drops off the bill, takes the money, and at the register, deeply investigates it. She checks it with a marker, holds it up, and calls someone over to look at it. She brings me back the change and leaves with a simple, "Thanks."

Nobuyuki watches her leave. "What did you do to her?"

"Not sure. I was checking out the money. It's been my first chance to look at it. I can't tell if they're like what I've seen in the past. She probably thought I was passing counterfeit bills."

Nobuyuki laughs. "Let's go look at clothes."

We get to the store ten minutes before they close. The employees seem deflated when I walk in. Probably a slow night and they're ready to flee.

We move to the Men's section and I look at dress pants, nice shirts, jeans, underwear, a couple of T-shirts. The employee locks the door.

"I'm going to try these on," I tell Nobuyuki and head out for the dressing room. Everything fits fine, but new clothes feel weird. I'm looking at my shoes, knowing I need to get something better.

I walk out and find Nobuyuki talking to someone. She puts her hand up. "Take your time, I'll stick around." I give the clothes to Nobuyuki and go look at the shoes. I barely hear Nobuyuki's conversation with the lady and hear the made-up story. We're new to the area. I just started a new job and needed some clothes. They walk back and look at more clothes.

I've got weird feet and always hated looking at shoes. I find some that I could wear at work and it hits me. We're settling here. No danger. No danger, except for the company I keep. I settle on the black sneakers and don't know what sort of dress code Marty has set up. I think he'll be comfortable as long as I don't show up in ripped jeans and a concert tee.

The light songs they have over the loudspeaker isn't anything I recognize. Every new world has new music and I've missed taking the time to listen.

Nobuyuki and the lady are near the register. Our piles have grown. "I found some new clothes too," Nobuyuki says. The lady rings up our purchase. The total seems low. Nobuyuki smiles at me and pays.

"Good luck to you in Fort Wayne." The lady says as we take our bags.

"Thanks." I'm thinking about wearing the new shoes out, but don't want to break them in on the walk home.

We leave the store and hear the lock click behind us. Within moments, the lights are off and we see the lady walk to her car. She drives off in the direction opposite of where we're going.

"Am I going to need a driver's license?" I ask. "Spring walks are fun until it rains."

"I'll look into it," Nobuyuki says as she's looking around. "I can't look up interdimensional refugees seeking driver's license and find out how to do it. Might need to make up some things."

We walk out of downtown. It's misting and there's lightning off in the distance.

"Yeah, a driver's license would be nice, so would a vehicle other than an interdimensional trash cart."

"That would cause some odd stares on the daily commute. I'll work on it tomorrow and see what I can find."

We make it to our neighborhood when it rains. We pass a fence and a dog barks. Nobuyuki drops the bag and suddenly reverts to her three-tailed fox form.

"I'll meet you at the house." They run off into the night as I scoop up their stuff. Nobody is out in the rain, so I think we're safe. They scored pretty big from the geek store. Several T-shirts and a pair of printed jeans. The rain pours when I hit our street. She's back into her little girl form, standing at the doorway under the porch, watching me walk and carry her stuff.

"Thank you for your help," I say when I hit the porch. I'm soaking wet and so are the bags. She takes the bags and comes back out with a towel. "I'll get everything washed and hung up. Go relax."

"So, what is it with dogs?" I ask while drying off.

"They are a natural predator. If one barks near us, we lose all concentration and revert to our natural form. I also don't like them."

"But I want a dog."

"You'll settle for a cat."

"I don't like cats."

"You don't know that."

I settle back in the easy chair and stare at the wall while Nobuyuki grabs hangers. This easy chair is fighting me, and it wins. I fall into a deep sleep and my day is playing back. The victory in the office, the meeting with the lawyer, I'm walking out of the building.

Someone is watching my memories and I can't stop them. I remember the abyss Tom showed me at the park and my dreams go dark. Something kicks my foot. The old man is staring at me and looking tired.

"Hey, past bedtime. You fell asleep."

I let out a groan before making my way to the bedroom. My shoes come off, and I fall into bed. I'm asleep before the lights go off. My dreams start again. The Michigan Power Center frames the dream. I stand outside the building and smell the atmosphere of downtown. Something tries to fast forward the day and I anchor myself to the spot taking in every minute detail down to the cracks in the sidewalk. Sancho Tom's Taco Truck is there, but I refuse to look at it. Suddenly, I'm back in the plague park looking at the holes in my memory. Darkness takes over, and I feel like I'm in the